The Physician's Arrangement

TC Camille

Published by TC Camille, 2021.

THE PHYSICIAN'S ARRANGEMENT

First edition. December 6, 2021.

ISBN: 979-8215500514

Written by TC Camille.

Table of Contents

To writing in a freezing apartment and the X-Flies. Thank you
to Hank.

The Physician's Arrangement
by
TC Camille

TC Camille

1

TC Camille © 2020

2

Chapter One

"Henry wait!" Beatrice shrieked not caring about disguising her voice. Her hands tremoring against her hips. Henry stopped in the doorway turning to face Beatrice. His figure fills the frame, imposing and towering above her own stout and stocky frame.

"This is the last time I offer."

"Henry please there is a way we can solve this." Her eyes darted around, the stress growing. She was ruined. Done. Dead.

"No. I made my offer; you made your choice."

"Henry please." She begged feeling to air leave her lungs as she collapsed, "You don't have to do this."

"Neither do you."

~

"Stop, that you look ridiculous."

Beatrice's hands ceased their thrumming on the book she held. Aunt Liana cast her eyes down at her. "You are a disgrace enough without your silly habits." Her aunt snapped her fingers in her face drawing Bee's eyes to her own. "With your father's death you became my responsibility. And by extension my husband's. You have brought enough shame on your own family name you will not bring any to mine." He aunt grasped her fluttering hands in a painful grip. "You will put these silly notions from your head. You will be married and become a dutiful wife and should you continue down the path you are on you will regret it. I promise you that."

Beatrice shifted her gaze, watching as the Scottish countryside passed in the window. She switched to curling and rolling her toes. Flinching as Aunt Liana swiftly stomped on her foot. Her brain kicked into motion. She was going to get out of here. Even if it ruined her. She was going to get out.

~

"Miss Grey! Miss Grey!" The sound of her name being shouted quickly pulled Beatrice from her thoughts. "Miss Grey." William Parcel quickly rounded the corner, flushed and out of breath. "Miss Grey, you must come quick!" Beatrice shot up.

"What is the matter Mr. Parcel?"

"It's one of the cavalry boys Ma'am. He just got himself kicked in the head by a horse."

"In the head? Bloody Christ." William Parcel, a secretary in the employment of the 6th Dragoons, quickly lead Beatrice from her spot in the park next to the military encampment a short way outside of the city. Brighton was one of the last stops for soldiers before their final destination of France and the far war-torn European shores. It was in that encampment that Beatrice had found her employment. And no. It was not in that way. She served as a sort of makeshift nurse. Handling the less dire cases in hopes to relieve pressure from the army surgeons. Which is how she spent most of her days, reading and sketching beneath an Elm tree a short distance outside of camp waiting to be called in.

It was also how she had made the acquaintance of the sweet William Parcel who she now followed. She followed swiftly behind him, weaving her way through the ocean of tents. She shot a glare at a man as he wolf-whistled as she approached the grazing fields. A small group of men were gathered in a circle, a circle Bee realized, containing another.

The group parted as she approached, some with respect, others leering. The man in the middle was seated on the ground clearly dazed. Bee gently kneeled next to him. "Hello there soldier." He looked up at her, her concern grew as she watched the man struggle to focus his gaze. "My name is Beatrice Grey; I'm going to help you with your head if that's alright." The man took a moment to understand the meaning of her words before nodding.

She carefully turned the man's head, seeing the impact print of the horse's hoof had made. She reached into her medical box, working quickly. She cleared the dirt from around the wound before moving to carefully clear the blood. A small crowd had gathered around her, coming to see her work. Her existence in the camp was quite the spectacle. To the men she was either a fool or a saint. A godly and caring woman or a manipulative soon to be whore. But the one thing that was not disputed by anyone, was that she was a help.

Well almost everyone. Several of the newer physician's had yet to come to respect her. Something that was a great hindrance to her work. The fact of which was proven as one of the physicians approached. "Get back you silly woman. The man needs the care of a proper physician not a nurse."

"Doctor he is quite alright," Bee moved just slightly to the side. Refusing to give up her spot at the soldier's side but allowing the man to see. "He is a little dazed, but he's still aware."

"Does he need to be bled?"

"No, it's small cut to his scalp, nothing more." She asserted; her annoyance grew. Every second she spent proving herself and explaining to men that she knew what she was doing, was a second she could be helping.

She blocked out the crowd. Fingers working softly but deftly around the wound. Feeling for swelling or soft points beneath her finger tips. She smiled, grateful that she hadn't found any. They would have been indictive of a larger problem. She quickly bandaged the man's head. Telling the few men around him that he would be alright, dazed for a bit, but alright.

She rinsed her hands, and closed her box before rising. Throwing the strap of the box over her shoulder as she did. "Would the lady like an escort back to her lodgings?" One of the men in the crowd offered. Anything but innocently.

"No, I am quite alright but thank you, I'm sure you're all very busy with your military tasks."

"Never too busy for a woman that looks like you." Another man chimed in.

Beatrice cast her gaze to the ground, now aware and uncomfortable with the gazes of the crowd. "I am quite alright thank you, I know my way out and back to the city."

"Oh, you know your way around, do you? Well perhaps you should use that knowledge to pay me a visit sometime?" That drew a chuckle from the crowd that sounded more like the roar of a lion in Bee's ears.

"I said I am quite alright." With that Beatrice pushed her way through and hurried back through the camp. Her eyes on the ground and her fingers thrumming against her box comfortingly.

The walk back to the boarding house where she was staying was short yet tedious. Even when the weather was nice, she disliked the gravely path and the course mud it would turn to in the rain. Yet the house always provided a respite. Quiet and filled mainly with officers' wives it always provided a comforting aura. The smell of firewood and broth overtook her as she walked in the door every time, thawing her frozen body. That comforting aura however paused for a moment as the lady of the house approached her.

"Miss Grey."

"Mrs. Beckham."

"There is some post for you. As well as the reminder that I run a respectable house."

Beatrice raised an eyebrow, confused at what could have caused the woman's ire. She looked at the letter and saw. She unmarried and female, had received a letter from a man. Or at least addressed that way.

"My sincerest apologies for causing you stress. But the sender is my uncle."

Ms. Buckham gave a thin-lipped smile, "Then I believe it is I who must apologize to you Miss Grey."

"You are fully forgiven, after all you were simply looking out for your establishment."

Ms. Buckham offered a stiff nod before walking away, saddened Beatrice presumed, by the loss of grounds to evict her. Well, Beatrice thought, depending on the true author of this letter she may have them soon enough. It did not take a scientist to know that her aunt was most likely the sender.

TC Camille © 2020

Chapter Two

She was numb. Completely and utterly numb. Even her restless mind had quieted. She sat in the grass under the Elm. It tickled her cheek. She shouldn't have waited to open the letter. She should have opened it while she ate. If she had she could have fallen apart in her room. Instead, here she was. On her side curled into herself. Numb. And worst of all beneath the Elm she rocked. The self-soothing action she thought she had long grown out of. Or had phased out of. The adults of her childhood bullying it out of her. Yet here she was. She held the letter clutched in her hand.

And that was how Mr. Parcel found her.

"Miss Grey are you alright?" The concern in the boy's voice was touching and probably necessary given Beatrice's current state.

"I am quite alright Mr. Parcel, what do you need?" She sat up attempting to gather herself.

"Miss Grey, I hope it is not out of turn for me to say this but I don't quite believe you." Beatrice stopped rocking and let her hands flutter at her hips instead. She tried to smile, to reassure him and cease his prying. But with the quiver in her lips, it was anything but. "Miss Grey?"

"Oh, my dear Mr. Parcel I am afraid that you wouldn't be able to help me even if you knew." If she opened up to him, she might break. Right now, she couldn't afford to break. Not here.

"But if it is upsetting you, I wish to help. Who knows? Maybe I could help you in ways you don't know."

Beatrice smiled softly at his kindness, "Thank you Mr. Parcel but I am quite positive that you can't."

"Well, we won't know unless we try."

"Well. That is fair enough I suppose. I have just received word from my aunt. She is not exactly happy with what I am doing here so she has withdrawn her support."

"She has refused to help you with your living expenses?"

"Oh, she has done much more than that. She has fully disowned me. Denying me my inheritance from my father and dissolving my dowry fund."

Mr. Parcel's mouth opened into a soft O. "Miss Grey. I. I am sorry."

"It is what it is Mr. Parcel. And besides it is hardly your fault."

"Oh Miss Grey I." He stopped for a moment staring into space.

"Yes?"

A grin stretched across his face, "I have an idea."

"An idea?"

"Yes. Oh yes." The boy shouted in excitement. "Yes. I have an idea. A wonderful idea." He grimaced slightly at his words. "Well. An idea."

"Do share it then." Her curiosity had gotten the better of her Bee noted.

"If you marry then your aunt will reextend your financial support?" He questioned.

"Well, I suppose so. She hasn't made any mention of anything other than my need to return at once." *As well as the threat* Beatrice thought to herself.

"Do you know Captain Hashworth?"

"I have heard of him." Beatrice replied wearily. Captain Hashworth was the captain of the 6th Dragoons. Mr. Parcel was his secretary. So yes, she had heard of him. She had heard plenty about Captain Edmund Hashworth. He drank. Swore. Smoked. Gambled and whored. Whored with any woman he could. Whore or not. Married or not. He was not exactly the type of person that she wished to acquaint herself with.

"He is in need of a wife."

"I have just told you I no longer have a dowry." Beatrice voiced. The rest of her concerns remaining silent. Mr. Parcel was a kind boy, but perhaps too trusting. Yet it was not Beatrice's place to take his love for the Captain away from him. She did have to admit to herself that he was good to his men. That he cared for them and provided a role for the young Parcel that Bee was sure that he didn't always have. Nonetheless she was wary of the man and even more wary of his reputation.

"No, no you don't understand. He too has been cut off. Until he is married. That's where you come in."

"While I do not believe it would be difficult for me to get the Captain's attention, I do believe it would be difficult for me to gain the correct type of attention from him." She stated, hoping that she wouldn't need to be anymore plain with the boy.

"No. That's the genius of it. You both know. The Captain knows about your situation, or he will once I tell him, and you know of his. You two get married, your future is secure and he receives his inheritance."

"I am not so sure Mr. Parcel, and besides I believe that that is a conversation that should happen between the Captain and I."

"Why of course it should. Of course it should. But that means that you are considering it?" Beatrice hesitated, "Because I can at least propose the idea to him. And set up a meeting. Yes, a meeting. You two can talk about all this and become acquainted with one another it's perfect."

"Perfect?"

Mr. Parcel flushed and looked down. "Well. I am aware that it is far from the perfect situation. But it is better than your current one."

Beatrice sighed heavily. "A fair point Mr. Parcel. A Fair point. Fine then, arrange this meeting with the Captain. But." Beatrice started as the boy took off in the direction of the encampment. "Be very. Very clear as to what this meeting is about and the intentions. And, be very clear that should he refuse word of my situation must not get out. The men of the camp already throw themselves my way without word that I'm looking for a husband." Bee muttered the last part. Not that Mr. Parcel would have heard. He waved his hand in a short response to the first part of her sentence, running from her and leaving her to ponder what exactly she was thinking. Throwing herself into a marriage with the likes of a man like Captain Hashworth was far from a smart idea. She paced beneath the elm, hands fluttering as she thought. She wasn't quite sure what she was thinking but at this point what other option did she have? The one thing she now knew is that, now, she was far from numb.

Chapter Three

Arrogant. Or perhaps just bastard. Handsome, but far too aware of it. That's was the way she would describe the great Captain Hashworth. No, she thought as he looked her up and down, git. Just git. She grew restless under his gaze. They had been silent since they had been introduced. Mr. Parcel was giddy at their introduction glancing between the two waiting for someone to speak, having to be asked to leave so the two of them could speak in private. She had hoped that the captain would speak first. The corner of his mouth turned up as if he had read her mind. "Well then. I suppose we both know why we're here."

"I suppose so." Oh, definitely git.

"Well?"

"Do you want to sleep with me? And yes, I do mean in that way." Beatrice took a step back in shock. Surely, he had not just said that. Her mind filled with exactly what she wanted to say to this man. No. This git. To her dismay all she got out was a startled what.

"Do you want to sleep with me, and I'll add on, are you a virgin?"

Beatrice was sure her flush answered the latter half of the question, "I, what? No."

"No, you don't want to sleep with me? Or no you aren't a virgin?" He asked amused at her reaction.

"What exactly does that have to do with anything." She refused to answer his question.

"It has everything to do with anything. My family and more specifically my father is not stupid. And I'm assuming that yours is not either. So, there will most likely be checks that ensure this marriage is valid. Is. Consummated." Oh, how Beatrice wished she would stop gaping like a fish. "So, I am going to ask again, are you a virgin? Because if you aren't then wonderful there are ways of faking a consummation. But if you are, do you want to sleep with me because that is something that cannot be faked, I am afraid." Beatrice's entire face was on fire. Her ears and neck to. He cocked his head to the side. "I'm assuming from well," He gestured vaguely at her reaction, "That you are a virgin. So, I ask again do you wish to sleep with me?"

Beatrice finally found the movement to shut her mouth, simply staring at the man. "We have to sleep together?" She hated that her voice came out sounding choked.

"Well, it would only have to be once. For your, er. Deflowering. But it would ensure that no matter how much either of our families meddle it can't be undone." His eyes cut from hers to the ground. This was not how he normally engaged in this sort of thing. The feeling of awkwardness grew in the room.

"I see."

"Do you want to sleep with me?" He grinned teasingly. Hoping to push the awkwardness aside. To but the both of them at ease.

"Git." He grinned fully at that.

"Feisty. I love that in a woman."

"I can leave you know. Leave you to deal with this yourself."

"But you won't. And I won't leave either because neither of us can solve our problems on our own."

Beatrice had to concede to that point. "Rules."

"What."

"There need to be rules."

"Don't worry I'll be gentle." He teased. He watched the blush race across her skin once again.

"No rules regarding everything. After all, there need to be considering the agreement were making." The Captain nodded, signaling her to continue. "We sleep together. Once. Or when we need to avoid suspicion." He nodded, "and," She hesitated, taking a deep breath before putting as much authority in her voice as she could manage. "I am staying."

"I don't understand."

"I am staying. With the army, as a nurse."

"That's absurd-" There was no way in hell he was going to bring this woman onto a battlefield.

"If I wanted to be sent away, I would simply return to my aunt, the entire reason I am giving everything up is so that I can stay. I am staying, you are not sending me away."

The Captain considered for a moment before conceding, "Fine, but I have some rules of my own."

"Go ahead."

"We keep any extramarital affairs quiet. After all the two of us know we are not marrying for love, but to keep our story we must play the happy couple. Therefore, outside relationships stay quiet and hidden."

"Agreed." She shifted from foot to foot.

"That also means we also need to play the happy couple. I believe that it will take more from both of our families to accept this marriage as true than a letter. Especially since it is happening so soon to the both of us receiving the news of our ousting."

She cocked her head to the side in consideration. "Fair."

"We have a deal."

"We have a deal." Beatrice could have laughed at the absurdity of a handshake to celebrate a proposal. "Also, we marry in three weeks. I want the Bains to be read."

"Fine." He studied her. Beatrice stood in front of him. She was small, he noted. Much smaller than him. Her forehead just reaching his chin. She was chubby and rather plain he thought. She wore a simple blue frock with a pinafore. Her red hair pulled into a bun at the nape of her neck. A small halo of runaway curls framed her face. He smiled softly. He watched as her hands fluttered at her hips. He felt a soft tug of protectiveness at the nervous action. And a slightly larger tug of guilt. She was nervous because of him. But nonetheless she was to be his wife and he would protect her no matter what. While he wished to sit and talk. To get to know her better, he knew that in order to protect her at the moment he needed to leave. With a farewell and a soft bow, he left the tent leaving her to ponder what exactly she had just agreed to.

Chapter Four

Only two days had passed before she saw the Captain again, he approached as she sat in the boarding house eating her breakfast. "Come on." She raised an eyebrow, spoon midair "Come on, grab your coat." With that he left just as quickly as he had appeared. She moved quickly, but admittedly confused, meeting him outside. She searched for him only for a moment, he was not hard to spot. Even amid the red that had over taken the city he stood out in his uniform. Tall and slender he stood proudly next to a chestnut mare. Not a single black curl out of place. He looked like something straight of the lid of a biscuit tin.

"What is going on?" He moved to hoist her onto the mare. "Wait what is going on?"

He sighed, "We have to get married today."

"What?"

"Please stop asking that."

"What?" Beatrice asked pointedly cocking an eyebrow at him.

"We need to get married today; the general does not want us to wait. He has taken an interest in my recent engagement and wishes to see us married. At once." Another cocked eyebrow, "He says you are a fine nurse and does not want to see you a ruined woman. You are a help around camp that he doesn't want to lose. And he wants to make sure that I follow through with my word seeing as he thinks that I already have well." He waved his hand in her direction, "And wants us to marry. Today. Now. Seeing as we can't get a license after noon we need to hurry." he went to help her again, she startled slightly as he wrapped his hands around her waist. She was shocked that she could feel the warmth in his hands. Even through the layers she wore and his gloves. "So please. Get on the horse." She placed her hands on his shoulders, steading herself as he placed her on the horse with ease.

~

They rode to the courthouse and then to the church in silence. The wedding itself was a silent affair, the two of them only speaking when asked to by the priest. Even Mr. Parcel, who attended as their witness, was silent throughout the whole thing. The silence followed them from the church to the inn. It followed them up the steps and into her room. There it sat over them, engulfing the room, and crushing Beatrice.

~

"Tell me something."

"What?" Hashworth turned startled at the sound of well. Sound.

"I am starting to feel crushed, and when I feel crushed, I panic and when I feel panicked, I cry, and I'm assuming you don't want to deal with me crying so please Captain-"

"Edmund." He said softly.

"Edmund. Please tell me something about yourself. Anything."

He walked a took a seat at the vanity across from where she was sitting on the bed. He looked at her for a moment placing his elbows on knees. "My favorite color is yellow."

She smiled slightly, "Like a daffodil?"

"No darker, richer. Like honey."

"I believe that counts as a gold."

He chuckled softly, "Need to disagree with everything I say" He smiled at her "Tell me something about yourself Beatrice."

"No one calls me Beatrice. Just Bee."

"Bee?"

"Bee."

He carefully moved to sit next to her on the bed. Their shoulders brushed and the both of them tensed at the contact. "What is your favorite color? Bee."

"Blue, or green. Like the ocean."

He smiled, this time she felt the small huff of air against her face as he laughed. "Pretty." Bee's mind was whirling around, the crushing feeling gone now replaced by restlessness. She examined him as the silence fell again, almost like how she would a patient. Starting from the head and working downwards. He was handsome, she could not deny that. Dark curls surrounded his face, a striking contrast against his light green eyes. He has freckles she noted curiously, odd for someone of his status, she thought at first before remembering the time he spent outdoors as a dragoon. Their eyes met briefly as he did his own examination of her.

"So now we..." She trailed off.

She watched as he swallowed his Adam's apple bobbing, beneath his cravat. "Yes, now we. Yes."

He softly cupped her cheek, asking her for permission. With her yes, he leaned in kissing her gently yet firmly. With one had he held her jaw the other falling to her waist. Thumb rubbing softly as she tensed beneath his touch. He was a rather good kisser she admitted to herself. The kiss had grown more passionate as the two broke for air, his tongue delving into her mouth as her breath hitched. She reached up grabbing the lapels of his jacket, unsure of where she should place her hands. That had apparently been the right answer, his hand shifting from her chin to the back of her head, tangling in her hair. The hand on her waist bunching at the fabric of her dress.

Her own hands found his curls as his lips found her neck. She let out a slight squeak as his teeth grazed over her pulse point. She felt him smile against her skin, one hand moved to cup her breast while the others worked at the buttons on her dress. She placed a hand firmly against his chest "Wait." He pulled back looking at her concerned, "What's your horses name?"

"Daffodil" He answered half dazed.

"No, it's not."

"I suppose it is now. Are you okay?"

"Yes. I mean I'm just." She faltered unsure of what to say.

Edmund shifted to sit in the middle of the bed, "Come here." He gathered her into his lap, simply holding her. She tensed slightly at the contact before slowly relaxing in his arms. "Do you want to stop?"

"No. I just." Her hands fell to his shoulders to fingers drumming slightly against to wool of his jacket. "I am nervous and I don't know you."

"I broke my arm when I was seven, fell out of a tree. I didn't learn how to swim until I joined the army, in fact I was and still am slightly terrified of the water. And" He grabbed her hand curling it around a bit of hair at the nape of his neck. "If you pull this in the upcoming activities it will be to your benefit." She gave it an experimental tug, watching smugly as he took a breath, his eyelids fluttering, "Now I know that none of this is how you would like it. That you don't know me and I don't know you. But we can make this good. I'll make this good for you, which not many other men can say for your first time."

Beatrice pulled again this time drawing a muffled groan. "Alright. Anything else that can be used to my benefit?" He grinned pulling her into a rough kiss.

Dragging her bottom lip between his teeth he pulled back. "Believe me if you're doing something good, I'll let you know." He pulled her into another kiss, fingers working deftly to undo the buttons of her dress. She carefully pushed the jacket from his shoulders, and undid the buttons of his waistcoat as best she could. One of Edmund's hands had started to grope at her chest. His lips returning to her neck, now trailed their way across her collarbone. She pulled his hair. He smiled against her skin and nipped her collarbone in return. Her breathing increased as he trailed kisses across her breasts, sucking at the sensitive skin.

She removed his shirt. Or attempted to. The both of them seemed to forget the existence of the buttons at his wrists, both of them pausing for a moment and humorously undoing them before continuing. "See you know me." Edmund said in between kisses.

"I do?"

"You now know that all common sense leaves my head when I have a pretty woman in my arms."

Bee hummed into the next kiss, letting her hands roam the expanse of Edmund's stomach and chest. His muscles tensed beneath her hands. Goosebumps spreading across his skin at her featherlight touch. "So, I'm pretty?"

"Lovely especially when you're like this." He started on the laces of her stays.

"Like what?"

"Swollen lipped," He finished loosening it, "Panting." He tossed the stay aside, and rocked forwards. "And under me."

She glanced up at him, growing shy with the state of undress she was in. He was in. Hovering just above her. "Quite the flattery for a marriage of convenience." She deflected.

"What can I say? I'm a dutiful husband." He rid her of her stockings and began sliding his hands up beneath her chemise. His hands stopped as they reached her knees, looking to her for assurance. She nodded and slipped the chemise over her head, pulling in on herself with a mixture of cold an embarrassment. Edmund gazed at the sight before him. The expanses of smooth skin laid before him reminding him of the fact that still wore his pants. His hands flew to the rolls settled near Bee's hips, squeezing slightly. Half of him, half of him wanted to take her then and there. To mark every inch of skin in front of him to make her writhe beneath him, as his lips travelled over every velvet peak and valley. The other half, the other half knew what he needed to do.

As much as he wished to waste the rest of the day away with her beneath him, he knew that she was nervous. Nervous and in a marriage of convenience. He leaned forward kissing her softly, "It will be easier, still a pinch, but easier, if you've already found your peak." She nodded against his lips, one hand on his shoulder the other finding perch in his hair again. *Smart girl* he thought.

Her back arched as his mouth closed around her nipple, relishing in the feeling as he moaned around it as she tugged his hair. One hand remained at her hip, the other moving to cup her core. One of his fingers running softly through the slit. Spreading the growing wetness.

His mouth continued its onslaught of kisses and bites on her chest as he carefully slid his finger in and out of her. His breath caught and he openly moaned as the sensation of her hand tugging his hair combined with his name tumbling from her lips in breathy moans.

"Bee." He buried his face in her neck, finger working fast hoping to bring her to climax soon. "Oh honey Bee." The wanton moan she let out as he slipped another finger in resolidified his need to be in her. Now.

Bee was shamelessly grinding her hips against Edmund's hand. The feeling of his fingers moving in her, curled ever so slightly was dizzying. She was off balance and didn't know what to say, settling for chanting his name. Given the erotic promises he began to whisper in her ear he must have enjoyed the sound of it. "Edmund." She moaned kissing him, her breath hitching and stomach tensing.

"That's right Bee, that's right." He moved his fingers faster, his thumb finding the small bud he knew would make her fall apart. She cried out hips bucking against his hand. "That's right Bee. Right like that." He was panting too, his forehead resting on hers. He could feel her beginning to spasm around his fingers. She was close. Oh, she was close. She would finish around his fingers and then he would get to be inside her. He would get to feel how warm, how wet, how-

The door shot open with a crack. Beatrice let out a small shriek, that Edmund would have much preferred been of pleasure, and attempted to dive beneath the blankets. The problem being the both of them were lying on top of them. Edmund flipped his side trying to shield as much of Bee as he could from whoever had just entered.

Chapter Five

"I knew it!" Ms. Buckham yelled. "I knew it, and I will not have it under my roof." Edmund had been interrupted before. An angry husband, and angry brother, a fiancé. But never an angry landlady. And he must say he did not enjoy it, especially as they were just reaching the good part.

Bee on the other hand was mortified. She greatly appreciated Edmund providing her with some cover as she struggled with the blankets before slipping beneath them. "I knew it. I knew it you whore I want you out of my house this instant!"

"Wait it's not what it looks like."

Even Edmund turned to her with a raised eyebrow, wondering how exactly she planned to rectify the situation with that statement.

"Then what exactly are you doing here, hmm?"

"No, I mean we're married. No whoring just consummation."

Edmund caught her meaning, "Yes no whoring here." he added.

"You are not married you, you slut."

"Actually, we just married this morning." Edmund added. The landlady's eyes, and anger, turned to him.

"Is that so?"

"Yes." The both of them answered. "and I would greatly appreciate it if you refrained from calling my wife a whore." Edmund added. Bee lightly swatted his chest.

"Then you will not mind me checking with the courthouse?"

"No?"

With that she turned on her heel and left determined in her new task. Edmund looked down at Bee, who had turned a lovely shade of pink, sat huddling beneath the blankets.

"That took any desire you had to finish this didn't it?"

Bee smiled sheepishly, "If she heard then most of the house heard."

"Most of the house is empty." He offered.

"Ah yes how could I forget; the officer's ladies must be away at tea."

"I hate to be the one to break the news to you but you are an officer's lady now."

"No thank you." Bee said softly burrowing further into the blankets. Edmund rolled onto his back, trying to get comfortable beside her, a feat in the small bed. He settled with one arm across his chest and the other thrown to the side over Bee's head.

"Oh, but you are one now. You'll spend you day at teas and in salons, chatting about the latest gossip and London fashions."

Beatrice glared at him, "I'll be spending my days the same way I did before. Waiting for medical emergencies beneath the Elm."

"And spending your nights at the boarding house or tent, in pleasure with your loving husband." That earned him an elbow to the ribs which he smiled at. The two lay in silence for a moment catching their breath, and calming themselves. Beatrice was the one to break the silence.

"We should get dressed and go before she gets back."

"Go where?"

"I'm not sure but anywhere is better than being here when she gets back." Edmund raised an eyebrow confused, "That is unless you want to wait around for an interrogation."

"An interrogation," Edmund muttered "We should probably prepare for that nonetheless, I'm sure that many people will have questions."

"We met at camp I patched you up from a fall, you instantly became infatuated with me" Bee swung her hands around in mock dramatics, "Eventually I caved to your advances. We decided to keep things quiet until the marriage."

"A compelling and romantic story. But with a rather large plot hole, why would we stay quiet until the marriage?" Bee considered for a moment before shrugging. He watched her hands as they fluttered around her hips, she noticed his staring and laced her fingers together to still them. "Sorry. I did not mean to stare."

"That's alright, it's just a silly habit. I do it when I'm anxious."

"Anxious?"

"Yes. Anxious." Her hands started fluttering again.

"What do you have to be anxious about?" For a moment she looked at Edmund like he had six heads.

"I'm in bed. Naked. With a man."

Edmund was up and moving around gathering their clothing. He tossed Bee her chemise. "That man is your husband."

"Whom I met two days ago." He hummed in response. The two of them began moving around the room gathering their things.

Edmund held out her hat as the two of them readied to leave. Accepting her thanks with a small wave of his hand. They descended the stairs together, Edmund offering Bee a comforting squeeze of her hand as they passed the parlor. Inside sat a small group of women, they chuckled and spoke behind their fans as the pair passed.

"Don't pay them any mind."

"Easy for you to say, you aren't to one they're laughing at."

~

Her hands fluttered. Her toes scrunched. She lightly clacked her teeth together. Edmund noted each of her nervous behaviors. He didn't care for her. He didn't. But he did like her. She was sweet, kind, and headstrong. And also, most importantly, his responsibility. He didn't care for her, but he would take care of her. After all he swore before God he would. She was his wife and he would care for her. And if that meant killing the man in front of him then so be it.

Bee had been the subject of camp gossip for some time, their marriage simply adding fuel to the fire. But of course, the Sargent in front of him had to push things too far. He was claiming loudly. Publicly. That he had *known* Beatrice. Even going so far as to ask how

Edmund liked his leftovers. All of this of course without realizing the happy couple stood right behind him. Without realizing that the husband of the happy couple was ready to finish him.

"Sir, I politely ask that you refrain from slandering my wife in public, or at all." Edmund spoke up, drawing the attention of the crowd. Bee tightened her grip on his arm, trying to pull him away.

"My apologies." The man smirked and winked at Bee, "that this as how you had to find out."

Edmund gave a brief wolf like grin. "Name your second." Bee smacked his chest and glared up at him earning hoots from the crowd. Edmund caught her hand and held it. He watched as the smile fell from the man's face. He must have finally realized the true nature of his mistake.

"Edmund please." Bee pleaded, "Let's just continue walking."

"He insulted your honor. As your husband I can't let that slide."

Bee smiled at him, almost threateningly, "I would also like for you to be my husband for longer than a morning. Something that goes against dueling."

"I would listen to your husband Lady Hashworth." A man made his way through the crowd. He stopped behind the pair, "The man has paid you great insult."

Edmund smiled at the man, "General Jensen. How are you today?"

"I fair quite well Hashworth, though I suspect your day might be fairing differently?"

"It has been eventful." He admitted, "General, may I introduce my wife? General Jensen, this is Lady Beatrice Hashworth."

"Lady Hashworth, lovely to make your acquaintance. Apologies but I must speak with your husband."

"Lovely to meet you General, and no need to apologize. This is a time of war after all."

"That it is."

Edmund turned to her, "I'll meet you back at my tent." He lightly kissed her forehead, an act which startled her slightly, and walked away with the general.

Chapter Six

She looked at the assortment of items around the tent. Trying to gain any insight into the man she had just married. The tent was clean, but lived in. There wasn't much in the it yet it was cramped. A small cot was in far left corner. The blankets pulled up but left unmade. At the foot of it lay a chest that looked as if it had sat open for some time, clothing spilled from the top. The rest of the chest was filled with books and trinkets, haphazardly thrown into it. A small table sat on the right side, a shaving kit and portable writing desk sat on top. She took a seat at the small chair in front of it. She drummed her fingers across the creaking wood, startling slightly when Edmund marched in throwing the tent flap open with a smack. He looked annoyed.

"So, you found your way here?"

"Yes, without your help I might add." He simply hummed, clearly far away from their conversation. "Is everything alright?" Bee questioned.

Edmund placed his hands on his hips and looked down at her, "No. Not exactly." He crossed the space and perched himself on the edge of the cot. "I'm leaving."

"What?"

"For France. That's what the General wished to speak to me about. The 6th Dragoons will be leaving aboard a ship, headed for France. My men and I will be leaving." He watched as Bee's hands began their fluttering again. Her eyes darted around. The tug at his heart returned. "Bee are you alright?"

"I'm fine just making my list. I'll need supplies, better to stock up here. Easier. I'll also need to find a pair of boots-."

"Boots? For what?"

"For walking of course."

"Walking?"

"Yes, in France."

"No, no. Absolutely not." He stood and began to pace. A difficult task considering the size of the space. He could barely take three steps before turning.

"What do you mean no?"

"No, you aren't going to France. Are you mad?"

"Where else am I going to go?"

"I'll write to my sister. Yes, I'll write to my sister you can stay with her."

"Absolutely not." Beatrice stood facing him, "We had a deal. You don't send me away and I continue to be a nurse."

"Yes. Here in Brighton. Not in France. Not on a battlefield."

"Yes, in France and yes on a battlefield-."

"No."

Beatrice looked at him incredulously. He stood in front of her with a stern look on his face. His hands were on his hips and he was clearly using his height to tower above her. Bold of him to assume that would work. "Yes. We made a deal. We agreed to the rules."

"That agreement ends at the French coast."

"There were no terms to our agreement."

"Well, there are now."

"No, there aren't. And a breach of the agreement means I can leave. So let me remind you that you need this marriage as much, if not more than I do."

"You can't leave we're already married."

"Not truly."

"Meaning?"

"Our marriage has not been consummated; I simply leave saying that I've had a change of heart."

"You need this marriage too."

"I can disappear if I want to, I've done it before I'll do it again. It's not hard to remake oneself in America."

"Then why marry me in the first place?"

"Because I care about being a nurse and I care about what I do. Now you send me away, I walk away, leaving you without a damn thing." He glared down at her clearly angry with the points she had made.

"Fine." She smiled pleased she had won, "But. We make this thing real. You don't get to leave once we get to France." She started to speak, "No, you said it yourself, you can step out anytime I need assurance that you won't."

"Fine." She pushed him away, "But, it happens in France. You said it yourself, you can send me away."

"The ship. I can't send you away and you can't run off."

"Fine."

"Fine."

"So, like I said I'll need a pair of boots." Edmund's lips drew into a thin line, he turned and returned to his place sitting on the bed. He sighed and placed his head in his hands, running his fingers through his hair.

"You would have fared better as a lawyer than a nurse."

"I know."

~

Two weeks later Bee and Edmund stood on the docks, waiting their turn to board the ship. Bee watched as the ship was loaded, the supplies, the horses, the men. One by one they all boarded the ship headed for a warzone. Most interesting of all, to Beatrice at least, were her fellow camp followers. The small band of women she was now a part of. As Edmund's wife she had a small number of privileges, small. She was granted her own cabin, well, Edmund was, she was allowed to share it. She was granted a wagon, which she denied. And she was granted to bring a lady's maid. Yet again she denied. Much to Edmund's annoyance.

Their happy couple facade was quickly fading. He clearly held a grudge against the fact that she was here. She decided to hold a grudge right back. About what? she wasn't sure. But when he began to act cold to her, she decided to act cold right back. However, the sourness behind their cabin door was beginning to seep into their charade outside of it. So much to the point that the other women in her small band began to offer her advice. Which she despised. She did not need to be told what to do in bed. Or how she should speak to her husband. On top of it all the sourness inside the cabin also made Bee increasingly anxious over the quickly approaching consummation. Leave it up to a physician and a Captain to create a set date for such a thing.

Chapter Seven

Beatrice slammed the door of the berth shut. Hoping that this time it would stick, two days into the journey the damned thing had broken. Leave it to her luck to cross the English Channel during one of the worst storms its seen in years. She wished to do nothing more than sleep, but she couldn't. Oh no she couldn't. For tonight was the night. The night when she became a wife. That is if her dear loving husband ever decided to show. It was nearly three hours since the time he normally returned. And Bee had stayed up the whole time, waiting and listening to that damned door creak and break loose. And when he did decide to show? He had the audacity to look happy.

"Evening Bee. How was your day, my lovely wife?"

"Wonderful. I got to spend the day knee deep in seasick soldiers."

"Lucky them they had the best nurse to care for them." He changed to his nightshirt, toed off his boots and climbed into bed next to her. Then. Then he had the audacity to try and kiss her. She turned her head, rejecting him and glaring at the confused look that crossed his face. "Is everything alright Bee?"

The only thing this man had was the audacity, "No everything is not alright. You treat me coldly for days on end and all of a sudden, you're kind again? And to top it all off I am exhausted, and you have the audacity to be late."

"I apologize for my behavior; however, I was not and still am not a supporter of you being here. My apologies if I took that out on you. I also apologize for my lateness, there was trouble with the horses, I should have sent a man to let you know that I was going to be late." He stroked her hair, an act which caused her traitorous heart to flutter. "And if you are exhausted, we should sleep. I know we set this date but we can wait."

Her face did not soften as he expected it to, instead it twisted up with more anger. "No, we set this date, this is happening tonight."

"You're tired-." He was cut off as she reached for the nape of his neck and pulled him into a kiss. "Are you sure?"

"Yes." She pulled him on top of her kissing him again. He settled himself between her legs, rolling his hips satisfied with both the jolt of pleasure he felt and the moan that tumbled from Bee's lips. He undid the buttons of her night gown, pushing it down one shoulder and caressing the breast that was exposed. She arched into him as he began to roll her nipple between his thumb and fore finger.

"It'll be easier if I bring you to your peak first, remember?" She nodded against his lips. He ran his tongue along her jawline, kissing and nipping down the column of her throat. He closed his mouth around her nipple, caressing the small bud with his tongue. He hummed as she began to mewl. He reached between their bodies and pulled her skirt up around her hips. He released her nipple with a pop and returned his lips to hers. His finger began with its small strokes again. He slipped his finger in, then another, curling them slightly. He pulled back looking at Bee's face as he pumped his fingers in and out. Grinning as her face scrunched in pleasure. Moaning as she pulled roughly at his hair. He stopped his movements briefly, grin growing as she continued to move her hips against his hand. She began to spasm around his fingers, breath hitching. He pulled her gown over her head kneading one breast with his free hand. He pulled back just as she was finishing, pulling his shirt over his head. He pulled her into a rough kiss, grinding his hips down against hers. He relished in the way his cock slid between her folds, coating it with her wetness. He bit at her neck, one hand finding its way to her hair the other returning to her breasts.

"Edmund, Edmund please." she cried out. Her head was buzzing with pleasure. He hummed.

"Tell me what you need. Tell me what you want honey Bee." The friction from his hips just wasn't enough. She arched into each spot where he touched her, chasing her release.

"You. I need you. Please Edmund." He moaned into her chest. One hand slid to her hip, the other going to position himself. She felt a slight pinch as he began to enter her, the pleasure of him filling her quickly pushing it from her mind. He rolled his hips against her going deeper with each thrust. His jaw had gone slack and his eyes fluttered shut.

"Oh, honey Bee. Oh, dear little honey Bee." He moaned as his hip bone ground against hers. He went slow, like he said he would. He moved in her with long deep strokes. She was in the clouds, hips rising to meet his with each thrust. The sensation of his thumb rubbing slow circles on her hip kept her grounded. But not for long. When his mouth returned to her breasts the same time his thumb reached between them to find that small bud she was gone. Wanton moans spilled from her lips. His name being called out as a plea filled the cabin.

It was all too much for him. The feeling of her finishing around him, the noises she made and the deathlike grip she had on his hair brought him tumbling over the edge with her. His thrusts became erratic his moans joining hers as he finished. He thrusted several more times riding out his high before pulling out and collapsing on top of her.

She could feel his breath across her skin as he lay panting on top of her. She hummed and buried her face in his curls. His thumb continued to draw small circles on her hip. She felt his lips brush her collarbone softly. He lifted his head up to look at her, rolling off of her slowly. "Are you alright? I didn't hurt you?"

She shook her head, "I'm alright. It didn't hurt too much."

"Good, good." She felt him smiling softly against her neck. She made a sound of confusion as he giggled slightly. He softly kissed the shell of her ear, whispering, "Next time we get in an argument I'm reminding you that I took your virginity." She elbowed him in the ribs softly, with no malice behind it. He rolled next to her gathering her in his arms. She slowly nodded off to the feeling of his breath in her hair and his thumb on her hip.

Letters From July 15th Through November 5th 1809

My Dear Niece,

It is with great regret that I write to you today. We have recently learned the dismal news of your refusal of Mr. Hanover's proposal. We have also learned of your relocation to Brighton. I must say that your father would be greatly disappointed with the spending of your inheritance in such a manner. Due to this disappointment, I am writing to inform you that you must return to us with great haste. I shall take full control of the spending and allocation of your inheritance. It shall remain under my control until such a time where you are married after which control over the funds shall transfer to your husband. I again write that you must return with great haste to avoid further ruin to your reputation as well as the family's. If you do not write of your departure or plan to return within the month then a permanent freezing shall be placed on your funds. As well as your disownment and dissolvement of your dowry fund. With this in mind, I expect to receive word from you soon.

From,

Your loving aunt and uncle

Duke and Duchess Chamberlain.

My Dearest Aunt and Uncle,

I write to you with happy news. I shall not be returning to you, instead I am traveling from Brighton on to France and the European wars. I understand that this most likely comes as a shock to you. However, after speaking about the matter with my husband it was decided that I will be accompanying him. As for my inheritance and dowry funds both can be sent forward to Baron James Hashworth. My husband's father and proprietor of the Hashworth estate. Your response to this letter can be sent along to his Royal Majesty's 6th Dragoons. The letter can be addressed to either myself or my husband, Captain Lord Edmund Hashworth. I also write to you thankful for allowing me to employ Mary Smith in my services as a lady's maid. I understand that her service comes at a loss to your household and thank you for the sacrifice. I hope you all remain healthy and well. You shall remain in my prayers and I eagerly await your response.

From your loving and dutiful niece,

Lady Beatrice Hashworth.

My Dearest Son,

I write this hoping that you receive it in France. I have received your letter informing me of your marriage. I have had brief correspondence with Duke Chamberlain your new wife's uncle. I wish you well in France.

Your father,

Baron James Hashworth the Second

Chapter Eight

Bee doubted that the chill would ever leave her skin. No matter how many layers she wore or how much heat she tried to sap from Edmund she could never seem to get warm. She shifted in his arms, wrapping her legs in his. He groaned in his sleep as she burrowed closer to him. She was wearing two pairs of stocking, a night dress and a shift as well as a woolen shawl. She was also wrapped in Edmund's arms, and as close to his chest as she could get. Yet the damp cold of the camp still crept in.

They had arrived at the encampment the night before. Or the morning depending on how you chose to look at it. All of them exhausted and cold. Tents were pitched, cots made and everyone was asleep long before their heads hit the pillows. Everyone but Beatrice. And she didn't get any. Or maybe she did, all she knew was that her head was pounding when the camp sprung to life. Her head was pounding and Edmund woke up and smiled at her. Her heart and hands fluttered and the day started.

~

"You look tired Lady Hashworth. But after all what can be expected? Cavalry captains know how to ride long and hard." Captain Fredricks of the 8th artillery laughed as Bee blushed and Edmund's hand tightened around his tea cup. "But Captain I also expect that you should know when to let a well ridden nag rest." Oh, Edmund was going to hit him. He turned his head slightly towards Bee and shot her an apologetic look. She let her hand flutter at her hip for a moment before it returned to the tea cup in front of her. She wanted out. They had gone to meet a friend of Edmund's father. Make a good impression, be mentioned in a positive light in the man's next letter to him. Or at least that was the plan.

Instead, they sat through comment after comment and joke after joke. Bee had already abandoned the tea in her cup, letting it grow cold. But she clutched the fine China like it was a life raft in the middle of the stormy sea. Edmund lightly knocked his knee against hers, letting her know he had seen her signal that she wanted out. Their little routine was down to a science now. After several meetings with officers and gentry they both knew each other's signals to leave. If Bee fluttered her hands or began shifting her feet Edmund knew to begin looking for an out. If Edmund's shoulders tensed or he curled his hands into fists Bee knew to feign illness or discomfort about the topic of war and battle. Bee didn't begin to panic and Edmund didn't throw punches. The perfect plan.

Or, near perfect. Edmund had tried several times to find and exit for the two of them yet Captain Fredricks was relentless in his hospitality. And his comments that made Edmund day dream of knocking the man out of his fine plush velvet chair. Bee began to wonder if she should fake a swooning as the Captain launched into a discussion on how Edmund should "remove himself quickly before the end." in order to prevent a pregnancy. As he talked about how of course Edmund would "miss the pleasure of seeing his woman filled" Bee was sure he was going to shatter the tea saucer in his hand. Bee watched as Edmund's head snapped towards the Captain and decided that a swoon was probably their best option.

Edmund beat her to it. With one swift motion he placed his tea on the table, sat back and brought his leg to rest on his knee. "Captain, I apologize. We have spent so long talking of my happy matrimony that I forgot to congratulate you on your son's." Bee watched the Captain's face fall slightly before being replaced by the mask of society that matched Edmund's.

"Why thank you Captain." The man's voice had soured alongside his face.

"Why of course, such occasions should be celebrated." Edmund smirked slightly and with that the conversation quickly came to an end.

~

As the two walked back towards Edmund's tent. Their tent, Bee corrected herself. She questioned him with a look and a raised eyebrow. "His son ran off with a kitchen maid. His eldest and only son. It was quite the scandal." He explained with a small grin.

"Also, quite rude to bring up at tea time. Also, something that I'm sure has soured his image of us. Something that will reflect in his letter."

"Oh no. I doubt of us. Of me yes without a doubt I'll be receiving an angry letter from my father soon. But you Bee. You were the perfect image of politeness." She simply hummed in response. "Doubt me?"

"Doubt your judgement of the situation."

"Well even if my judgement is in doubt I stand by my actions." He pulled her back against him as a horse galloped past. "Mention my wife's moans at tea." She heard him mutter.

"Protective?"

He glanced down at her, "Of course I am, you're my wife." He scoffed. "Even if this is a marriage of convivence for us both your still my wife and your honor is mine to protect."

"With your life?" she teased.

"Of course." She expected a teasing tone back. The serious tone of his voice shocked her. The fact that he said it without hesitation or even a glance her way unsettled her. Her skin crawled as realization set in. The wounds she had seen and treated from duels had been some of the worst she had encountered. To many times had she needed to completely amputate limbs. Too many times of informing family members and watching men die painfully. All over affairs of honor.

"Don't." It sounded like a beg. It was a beg. She didn't care. She begged. That got her a glance. A hard one.

"Don't what?"

"Protect it with your life. I'd rather not see you shot in a duel. Don't think I've forgotten what happened in Brighton."

"Don't think that I have either. I swore in a church and before God that I'd protect you, and by extension your honor, with my life. I intend to keep that vow."

"Edmund." she scolded as they entered the tent.

"Bee." His response was short. Clipped. He was angry with her.

"Edmund. Stop. I'd rather have you alive and my honor scathed then you dead and my honor preserved."

"Well, I'd rather see you honor preserved."

"Edmund."

"That's the end of this discussion."

"No, it is not."

He turned towards her, "Yes, it is." He punctuated each word with a step towards her. "Your honor is mine to protect. If that means dueling over it then I will. There is nothing more to be discussed."

"Edmund-"

"Drop it. This conversation is done." He turned and sat on the cot opening a book. Bee watched him as he flicked through the pages. Arms crossed in front of her and eyes narrowed.

"Fine."

"Fine."

Chapter Nine

Bee had expected the hospital to be quiet before the battle. Afterall if there wasn't a battle the men wouldn't be getting hurt, right? She had been wrong. Oh, so wrong. The church turned field hospital was a hive of activity. Injuries from falls and accidents as well as drunken fights and plenty of duels had men streaming in and out. A nonstop flow of people. It both overwhelmed and excited Bee. It gave her a chance to practice and go over the basics. Stitching and resetting bones before the injuries became life threatening. It also gave her the chance to learn again. Something she was more than happy to do. Under the tutelage of Dr. Monty, she had learned much of what it meant to be a battlefield nurse. Well, field hospital nurse. Just when she had thought of forgiving and speaking to Edmund again, he had decided to drop that on her. Or Dr. Monty had. She found out that Edmund had taken it upon himself to speak to the Doctor on her behalf.

He had asked, no, instructed the doctor that she needed to remain back at the field hospital. That she wasn't to go anywhere near the battlefield. Not even to help transport the men back up to the church. This revelation from the Doctor had caused her to march straight back to their tent. And sparked another argument that Edmund refused to have. So, Bee went back to refusing to speak to him. Something that seemed to annoy him. Something that caused Bee to continue until eventually Edmund joined in the silence. Their arrangement of playing the happy couple had quickly been forgotten. Which caused Bee to learn another thing. There wasn't a single secret in the little circle of tents that she now called home.

Anytime she didn't spend in the hospital she spent with the other women in the circle. At first, she wasn't sure how she fit into the group. It was clear to her that the circle had a rhythm they fell into. It took Beatrice sometime before she fell into it as well. However, this had been a double-edged sword. On one hand, she was happy for the company, as well as the steady flow of work. After the long hours at the hospital, it was nice to come back to the calmness of the circle. While there was still work to be done back at camp it was calming to Bee. The mending and washing of clothes, cooking and the other tasks kept her hands busy. Sadly, it didn't keep anyone's mouth busy.

"I'm just saying my dear." Miranda Simms, the oldest and unofficial leader of the circle, said. "The silence you two have self-imposed will not solve your hurts."

Bee struggled with the thread in her hand trying to undo the knotted mess. "Hurts?" She scoffed.

Mrs. Simms took the thread and undid the knot with ease, handing it back to Bee. "Yes. Your hurts. Clearly the silent treatment is hurting the both of you."

"It very clearly is." Margaret Lanes added. Bee watched annoyed as the rest nodded their heads. She huffed and rolled her eyes, focusing on the ripped sleeve in front of her, her third attempted at fixing the torn shirt. She had always been better with flesh than with cloth. It looked like she was finally going to win the dreaded fight when Edmund brushed past her in all his pompous glory.

"Tent." She clenched her jaw. It was one of the first words he said to her in days and it was a command. Not a good start for speaking again.

"Talking will heal the hurts." Mrs. Simms chimed in.

Bee balled the shirt in her hands following him into their tent. Once there she launched the shirt into the chest. It slid down the lid and settled with a small plop.

"We need to talk."

Bee turned to him, straightening her back and lifting her chin. "We do." Edmund sat silent in the chair for a moment fiddling with the cuffs of his jacket.

Bee wasn't sure what she expected of the conversation. An apology, or even just ignoring the fight and beginning to talk again. Instead, it seemed like he had decided to pick another one. "I've arranged travel from here to the coast. Then to Brighton. My sister will meet you there and you'll stay with her while arrangements are made." He spoke quietly and refused to look up at her.

She stood shocked, "What?"

"In case-"

"We had a deal," Bee solidified cutting him off. "You. Don't. Send. Me. Away." She was pacing now, "What? We have one argument and you decide to send me away? No. No. You don't get to. That isn't fair,"

He grabbed her by the shoulders forcing her to look at him. "Look at me. I'm not sending you away-"

"Then what do you call this huh?"

"A back up plan."

"A back up plan?"

"Yes, if I fall in this battle, I'm not leaving you alone here."

Her anger calmed for a moment. He was just trying to protect her. She felt ashamed for a moment before her eyes narrowed. "When would I be leaving?"

"What?"

"When would I leave." He just clenched his jaw and looked at her. "Edmund. When would I leave?"

"The day after tomorrow" he said hoarsely.

Bee's eyes blazed, "Everyone says that the battle isn't for another week."

"Bee-"

"No. You're using this as an excuse to send me away."

His eyes softened and he cupped her face, "Bee."

She threw his hands back, "Don't. You never wanted me here so now you have an excuse to send me away."

"I'm not trying to send you away I'm trying to protect you."

"Protecting me." She laughed bitterly, "Protecting me. No. You want me gone."

"Bee. Please." He held out his hands. She didn't take them. "You're right I don't want you here, but I'm not trying to send you away. I'm not."

"Git."

Chapter Ten

A shell exploded over head.

Edmund laid with his back to hers. Since their argument they slept like that. Back-to-back. But neither of them slept that night. No one in camp did. The sound of shells bursting overhead kept everyone awake that night. The war had finally reached them. Tomorrow Edmund would ride out. Tomorrow she would stay behind and deal with the wounded and dying. Tomorrow she would wait to see if he passed through her hospital for her care. Tonight however. Tonight, it appeared that there would be no words between them. He had silently crawled into bed beside her. Mimicking the actions of nights before. She felt him shift beside her, shoulders bumping momentarily. He pulled quickly away. Both of them knew that the other was not sleeping. But both of them refused to replace the silence that had come to crush them once again.

A shell exploded over head.

For the thousandth time that night Bee repeated the passages from her medical book. She went over it all. Gunpowder burns, musket wounds, bayonet wounds, the splinting of every bone she could remember. She worked her way through the book. Once she had repeated that she started on what her father had taught her. Her father had taught her everything he learned from the revolution. The cures that weren't in the books. The ailments that went unmentioned. How to hold a man as they died, how to comfort them. How to bring them back as they drifted into their own minds. She ran through it all again.

A shell exploded over head.

She jumped slightly as the silence between them was broken. It was broken in the tiniest way possible. But the sound still brought tears to her eyes. Beside her Edmund prayed. She didn't hear for what or who but she heard her name and the Lord's. His soft whispers broke the silence. Her's joined in. She had not prayed in sometime. Her faith wavered as her life went on, seemingly without help from the great unknown. But she prayed, whispering Edmund's name and the Lord's. She made sure he heard.

A shell exploded over head.

Edmund rose from the cot and began dressing. She watched in the darkness as he did. Every single movement he made calculated and precise. He tied is cravat with precise care. The buttons of his waistcoat perfectly in the middle of the buttons on his pants. He pulled his jacket on, smoothing the creases and wrinkles. His boots, polished bright came next. A sound of a match lighting filled the tent. The soft glow of a candle on the table providing light. Their eyes met in the soft light of his shaving mirror. He broke it first, looking away and he closed the mirror. He strapped his sword to his side, and sat softly in the chair.

A shell exploded over head.

She rose. Pulling her stay over her head and tightening it. A cotton and wool petticoat followed, buttoned with care. Edmund's eyes followed her the whole time. She went to the small chest at the end of the bed and selected a brown dress from the small stack of her clothing that was piled neatly in one corner. She met his eyes again as she pinned the thick canvas apron on, pulling a shawl around her. He rose allowing her to sit in the chair. She loosened the plait in her hair, starting when he reached out to redo it. With all the care in the world he spiraled it into a bun and pinned it to the nape of her neck. Carefully securing the fly away auburn curls. They both stilled for a moment his hands coming to rest on her shoulders.

A shell exploded over head.

She reached up to grab his hands but he withdrew. When she turned to look at him, he was leaving with his saddle thrown over his shoulder. She took several deep breaths trying to calm the tears that were rising. She turned, grabbing her medical box, opening it to examine to contents inside. Her fingers moved deftly through it, ghosting over each item to ensure herself it was still there. She clipped it shut. Letting the noise echo.

A shell exploded over head.

She sent up one last prayer. Opening the tent flap, she walked through the silent camp. The faces of the women left behind stared at her as she walked. The weights of their gazes and of what she was going to do weighing her shoulders down. She would be the one. The one they cursed when their husband, brothers, fathers died. The one they praised when they lived. She entered the church turned hospital.

A shell exploded over head.

It had long since lost its sense of sacredness, its sense of holiness. The pews had been removed and added to the firewood piles. Their spaces being replaced by rows and rows of cots. At the alter turned surgical table Doctor Monty stood ready to make a twisted sermon.

A shell exploded over head.

A man cried out.

Her place in the battle, and in the history books was solidified.

A shell exploded over head.

The church doors swung open as men yelled.

A shell exploded over head.

A man collapsed in front of her bleeding.

A shell exploded over head.

She dove to catch him her hands becoming slippery with blood.

A shell exploded over head.

Her job began.

Chapter Eleven

The blood had soaked through her apron, through her dress and now clung to her skin. Her hands had started to waver. She knew. She thought she knew what she would see. What she would have to do. But living it was so much worse than imagined. The church was filled with the cries and moans of the dying. She moved swiftly between them, helping each man as best she could. She didn't know how she would feel as a battlefield nurse. But she didn't expect to feel like an angel of death.

Each man she passed looked at her the same way. Silently asking for answers she couldn't give. She applied bandage after bandage, salve after salve. Cared for head injuries, bone injuries, gunshots and burns. All the while the shells continued to explode. In the distance a horse whinnied and her mind jumped to Edmund. She pushed him quickly from her thoughts. The battle was coming to an end. They had won. But now the real work began. The men that couldn't return to the church themselves would be brought in. Carried in. Dragged. The last round of injured were always the worst. She couldn't think of him. Not now. She needed her head to be clear.

But as time went on her worry grew. Man after man passed through the hospital. Outside she heard cries of victory. Another wave of men rushed into the hospital. Healthy men. They hooted and hollered that they had won the day. They rushed through the hospital grabbing at their wives and the nurses pulling them into embraces with glee. Bee's eyes scanned the crowd. She didn't see him. Her hands fluttered at her hips for a moment and a tightness squeezed around her heart. Part of her worried that he was laying on the battlefield somewhere, injured and unable to cry for help. Another part of her brain, a terrible dark part told her that he was alright. That he simply didn't want to see her. As patient after patient continued to pass that small terrible part of her brain began to win.

Doctor Monty approached her. Telling her to return to her tent, to sleep. Her argument to stay fell on deaf ears. She knew she needed to sleep. The stress and fatigue of the day washed over her in waves. But she didn't want to go back to the tent. She didn't know if she dreaded it would be empty or filled. She thought as she dredged back through the mud. She decided finding it empty would be worse. She decided that living through years of the quiet that had grown over the space with him would be better than the quiet that would grow there in his absence. She dragged her feet as she walked, a mixture of fatigue and dreading her answer slowing her pace.

She never got the chance to find her answer. A horse came up behind her startling her. What startled her even more was when the rider dropped down on top of her. He nearly brought the both of them down into the mud, steadying them at the last moment. She panicked for a moment trying to throw the man off of her before the scent of Edmund's shaving cream hit her. He clung to her like she was his raft. He buried his face in her hair and held her tightly not wanting to let her go. She clung to him right back. Holding him as tightly as she could before the doctor in her kicked in.

She pulled back from him despite his protests. She looked him over, opening his bloody uniform and checking for injuries. She saw a few surface cuts but it was what could have lied beneath that worried her. He pulled her close again as she ran her fingers through his hair checking for head injuries. "Come on." He pulled her to follow him, he handed his horse off to Parcel and pulled her towards their tent. He pulled her down onto the cot, and held her close.

"Edmund, were both covered in blood and grime and I still want to check you for injuries." Bee protested.

"Shh, I just. I need to hold you." His voice was thick as he blinked tears from his eyes. She sighed, and clung to him right back. His lips brushed her forehead and she leaned into the touch. They stayed silent.

The silence was comforting this time, filled by the sound of their breathing. The assurance to the other that they were alive.

After a moment Bee pulled away. "Edmund, I need to check you for injuries."

"I'm alright, nothing bad."

"That is far from reassuring." She stood, heartbeat in her ears as he tried to stop her. To continue holding her close. He lightly held onto the skirt of her gown, a silent beg for her to stay. She grabbed her box and pulled the chair next to the bed. She ordered Edmund to strip off his jacket, waistcoat and boots. An order he was quick to follow. She did a once over of him. Checking for any cuts of blood, having him move each of his limbs. He wiggled his fingers and toes with amusement when she asked. She found nothing more than a couple scrapes and bruises that she cleaned with care. The whole time he watched her, eyes following her with a look that made it hard to meet his eyes.

"Beatrice? Bee? Honey Bee?" She flushed at the last one.

"Yes?"

"I." He paused for a moment. "Thank you."

She smiled softly at him, rejoining him on the cot. His arms pulling her close to him with the intent to never let her go. "No need. It's my job." He pressed another chaste kiss to the back of her head. She slowly drifted off in his arms. He spoke of nothing yet he was speaking. The sound of his voice a lullaby. She smiled against his chest and wished him goodnight. The silence was finally broken.

Letters from November 15th to November 25th 1809

My Dear Sister,

I hope this letter finds you healthy and well. You may have heard from Father that I have recently married. My apologies for not writing to you with this news sooner. However, I now ask you for a favor. While the chances for victory in this battle are high there is still the chance that I may fall. If I do I ask that you please take in my Beatrice until a time is made for further arrangements. I hope you and you children are well. Give my regards to your husband.

Your Brother,

Edmund Hashworth

My Dearest Aunt,

I hope this letter finds you well. I have awaited word from you about my marriage. I hope you and my dear Uncle have not fallen ill. A battle is approaching and I may not write for some time.

Your Niece

Lady Beatrice Hashworth

Chapter Twelve

It had been nearly a week since the battle but the army remained where it was. They were in no condition to continue marching. But that week had provided everyone with a much-needed rest. Almost everyone. For Beatrice and the rest of the nurses and physicians the work had begun to pile up. From the remaining wounded and injured from the battle to the new injuries that seemed to flood in everyday the hospital had been a non-stop hive of activity. It had meant many sleepless nights for Beatrice. And many lonely nights for Edmund.

His breathing was heavy as he palmed himself through his pants. His hips rocked at the feeling. He was pent up. He needed this. He groaned softly, undoing the buttons of his pants. He hesitated for a moment, no one was going to interrupt him. It was late enough that no one was about, yet early enough that the noise of the camp would keep him silenced. Besides even if someone was to interrupt, they wouldn't be walking into the tent unannounced. A small piece of guilt still weaseled its way to the front of his mind. He didn't know why. He'd done this before. Campaigns were long, lonely and cold. A man had needs. He had needs. Yet here he lay, feeling like a teenage boy about to get caught. He began stroking himself, groaning as he tried to push that thought from his mind.

He stretched, head rolling to the side as his hand moved at a lazy, unhurried pace. His movements ceased as his eyes fell of Bee's shawl draped over the back of the small chair. Was that why he felt guilty. This small tent was no longer just his. He shook that thought from his head. Bee wouldn't mind; besides she was at the hospital for the night. What she didn't know wouldn't hurt her. He focused on the canvas above him. He stroked faster, focusing on the pleasure, using it to banish his thoughts. He groaned through a clenched jaw, eyes fluttering shut. Bee's face flashed in front of him. Head thrown back in pleasure as she moaned his name. His stomach tensed and he pushed the image from his mind. It was replaced by her breasts, the skin soft under his hands, the warmth of her around him. He threw his head back, his jaw tensing and untensing. He groaned long and low, hand moving faster as he chased his release.

"Have you seen my shawl-?"

Edmund quickly flipped onto his stomach, trying, and failing, to regulate his breathing. To hide what he had been doing. He turned, a soft shade of pink had spread across Bee's face, traveling down her neck and to her chest. Her chest. The sight of her standing in front of him, breathless and chilled from the wind was not helping the situation. The two of them stared at each other for a moment, unsure of what to say. She had found her shawl, his brain noted. It was woven between her fingers. Bee opened her mouth as if she was going to speak before closing it and walking from the tent.

Edmund's brain had barely supplied him with a sarcastic *great* before she returned.

"Roll over."

It was not a request, rather a command. Edmund hesitated for just a moment before rolling over. One hand curled into his hair the other fisted in the blankets. A small line of defense against touching himself as she watched. Something he oh so desperately wanted to do. He lay flushed and breathing heavily as her eyes scanned his body. She had seen it all before. But that one time was different. She had tried to focus on everything else but him. Trying not to stare in the name of politeness. But now. Now. He was spread out on the cot, a mess and half ruined. Desperate. Her eyes traced their way back up his body. When they locked eyes, she moved. She sat lightly next to him on the cot. Her hand resting softly on his thigh. She felt the muscles in his leg tense. She went to remove her hand but met his eyes. From that single look she knew that they weren't tensing from discomfort but from need. Her hand slid slowly upwards, looking for any sign of disapproval, and came to rest at the juncture of his thigh.

Her thumb rubbed softly, drawing circles on his skin, mimicking his actions earlier. The both of them sat in silence, interrupted only by the sound of Edmund's heavy breathing. His eyes unlocked from hers for a moment to search her face. "Please." He hadn't meant for it to sound like a plea. But it was. A desperate plea that Bee was quick to answer. Her hand began to stroke his cock, feather light in its touch. He didn't bother quieting himself. His small gasps and moans filled the tent. Her grip tightened incrementally with each stroke, testing to see what was the most pleasurable for him. She knew that she found it when his hips snapped to meet her hands. "That's right honey Bee. Just like that." He was breathless. The words coming out in puffs. One of his hands remained woven in his hair as the other came to hold hers. He guided her hand up and down. Showing her how to flick her wrist. Eyes never leaving hers. He was going to fall apart. Soon. And judging by the way she was stroking him faster, she wanted him to. The sound of his needy moans filled the tent. They mixed with the light sound of "honey Bee" falling from his lips. His face contorted into a look of pleasure as he finished. His hips snapping up into her hand, her slowly stroking him through his release. His eyes closed; he felt her place her hand on his thigh again. After a moment he felt her rise from the cot and leave the tent. He opened his eyes again after she left. She forgot her shawl.

Chapter Thirteen

Henry listened closely to the man across the table from him. He was drunk. Messy drunk and ranting about a certain Cavalry Captain that Henry had a vested interest in. He poured the man another round. Angry men talk. Drunk men talk more. Angry drunks? The best thing Henry could have asked for.

"I don't get it. I don't, you see I was ruined; my wife was ruined. But oh no. Now the fine gentleman has the pretty little thing as his wife. And what? Because she's kind he's a good man? No. No. I remember what he is."

"I'm sorry my dear friend. Sometimes the world is cruel."

"No. No this isn't cruelty. This is plain and simple shit."

"Shit my friend shit." Henry clinked their glasses together and drank. Drank to the toast of shit. To the slandering of Captain Hashworth. And the memory of Bee.

~

Neither of them had discussed what had happened in the tent. There was an unspoken understanding of what transpired. What it meant. Just because it went unspoken didn't mean that it wasn't at the forefront of Edmund's mind most of the night. And the following day. Hell, it was all he could think of. Bee's soft eyes and her hand around him. He hadn't seen her since, she had spent the night in the hospital and remained there so far. After trying and failing to work on the letters and paper work he needed to get through he decided to go for a walk. Hoping the time away from the tent. The camp would clear his mind.

Naturally the world seemed to have other plans. He was annoyed at first when the man walked up to him. His annoyance only grew with the smug aura the man exuded reached him.

"Captain Hashworth?" The man that called for him was slightly shorter than Edmund. His blond hair was styled perfectly and he was dressed far to finely for a French battlefield. The very way he walked annoyed Edmund.

"Yes?" He raised an eyebrow at the man.

"I'm pleased to finally make your acquaintance. My name is Henry Jackson."

"Pleased to meet you Mr. Jackson now if you'll excuse me, I am very busy and I have things I wish to get back to." Edmund knew his behavior might be seen as cutting to the man but he wished for nothing more than to return to the solitude of his thoughts.

"I was actually hoping to speak with you. I was wondering if you could point me in the direction of Beatrice Grey. She is an old friend of mine whom I am hoping to reunite with."

Edmund felt a slight spark of jealousy before he tamped it out. He was sure the Bee would have mentioned something of that manner. At least after what transpired the night before. "Hashworth. She has married, her name is Beatrice Hashworth now. May I enquire as to who you are sir?"

"My name is Henry Jackson. As I stated before. Has she never mentioned me? Well, I suppose that makes sense. After all her marriage prospects were slim, a Captain and Baron's eldest son is quite the catch." The man spoke with a velvet voice, it was clear that lies slipped easily from his tongue.

"I'm sorry but she hasn't. And as for her marriage prospects I must say I don't know what you are talking about."

The man smiled at him and Edmund's irritation grew. "Now Captain we both know that isn't true."

"I'm sorry? I'm not sure I catch your meaning."

"Well, I mean we both know that her reputation was ruined when you two first met."

Edmund's lips drew to a thin line. He was not at all pleased with what the man was implying. Or the fact that he had the audacity to speak of it with him. "If you have something to say to me, I suggest you be frank."

The man looked at him smugness growing. "Oh, were you unaware? Well then, my sincerest apologies sir. But to continue and inform you, her reputation was ruined in well, the manner that many women's reputations are. And of course, there was the business of her becoming a physician."

"Oh, my good sir. But of course, I was aware that she was studying to become a physician. After all she is a nurse now and well." He stopped grinning. "I am also aware that you lie and are spreading rumors with the first accusation. Now I understand that you may have heard some rumors from the men but let me reassure you that they are false."

"Oh, but Captain. I know from my own experiences that I am not."

Edmund's hand shot out and grasped the man's shoulder. A friendly gesture to any onlooker but the tightening of his grip made it clear to the man that Edmund would not be playing this game. "And I know from experience that you are. Things like that are hard to fake and I suggest you stop concerning yourself with my wife's honor."

The grin slipped from the man's face. "She's slept with you?"

"Of course she has. I'm her husband. Which is also why I can tell you that her honor was intact when we married. And which is also why I am warning you that you should stop speaking on the matter." He turned to walk away before the man said anything else.

"No. I don't think I will." The grin on the man's face had contorted into one of rage. "You know nothing of the bitch that you call your wife. No one in this camp does. Consider what I will be telling people a favor so that you can soon rid yourself of the scheming whore." He called after Edmund.

Edmund spun on his heel and marched up to the man. "I warned you to shut your mouth. Name your second you'll be hearing from mine in the morning."

Mr. Jackson's eyebrows shot up, "A duel?"

"You imply you've slept with my wife, and call her a whore and a bitch and you're shocked that I challenge you to a duel."

"My apologies Captain but I came here hoping to have a civil conversation about Bee."

That was Edmund's final straw. "Don't call her that. You don't get to call her that. Her name won't leave your mouth again. You won't speak to her while you're here you won't look at her."

"Captain surely-"

"No. Name your second and leave my wife alone." Edmund turned and walked away fuming. He needed to find his wife. He needed to speak with her. Now. He made the trek up to the hospital, people jumping from his way. He was radiating rage.

Chapter Fourteen

It was not hard to find Bee once he entered the hospital. She greatly resembled her nickname. Buzzing from one patient to another. A smile on her face as she talked with each man. He swiftly walked to her. When he grabbed her arm, she looked up startled. Her expression quickly shifted to one of confusion and concern. "Edmund, is everything alright?"

"We need to talk."

"Well, I'm a little busy at the moment. Is it possible to wait?"

"No. We need to talk. Now." He began to pull her out of the hospital despite her protests. This wasn't a conversation that he wanted to have in public. He didn't even want it to happen in the tent. He would have preferred for it to not happen at all.

"Edmund what has gotten into you?"

"We need to talk."

She pulled her arm from his grasp, "So you've said. What do we possibly need to talk about that is so urgent you are pulling me away from patients?"

He walked close to her, lowering his voice. "We need to talk about your friend Henry Jackson who has decided to make an appearance."

He watched as Bee paled. His heart fluttered, his angry dissipating slightly. "Henry Jackson is here?" Her eyes were wide as she looked up at him. She was afraid. Edmund prayed that it wasn't of him. But considering the anger that he had portrayed he couldn't blame her if she was. However, the other option of her being afraid of Jackson caused his rage to spike again. He reached out cautiously lightly taking Bee's hand.

"Let's go back to the tent. We should talk." She nodded slightly taking his arm. Her hands fluttered against it. She was nervous. Anxious. And now he was too.

Her hands fluttered as she sat in the chair. Edmund sat across from her on the bed. He reached out placing a hand on her shoulder. His face was full of concern at her reaction but she wasn't sure how to comfort him. How to comfort herself. She looked at him full of worry. "What did he tell you? What did he say to you?"

Edmund hesitated. She didn't like that he hesitated, "He said a lot of things. Things about you and him." And this she let out a broken laugh, "Things about you becoming a physician."

She took several deep breaths taking his hands in hers. He squeezed her hands, holding on to her trying to become a raft for her. "Of course, he said those things, of course he did. Bastard."

"Bee? Is everything alright?" He questioned softly, "You seem afraid."

"I was trying to become a physician. I wanted to be one. But he stopped me. He ruined me." Edmund's hands tightened around hers, "Don't worry not like that." She paused taking a deep breath, he swept in thumbs over her skin. "Tried but never got the chance."

"Good." She squeezed his hands back. Taking comfort in the contact. He had started to become her raft and she couldn't be more thankful.

"He was teaching me. Helping me, he offered to open a practice with me. Imagine that the first female doctor in Philadelphia. With her own practice and partner."

"What happened?" He asked cautiously.

"He tried to blackmail me. Threatened me that if I didn't at least sleep with him, he would stop teaching me. He would send me out, leave me penniless if I didn't marry him. Slander my name in the gossip papers if I didn't sleep with him." Edmund's hands tightened around hers, "I'm sorry I didn't tell you. I know-."

"You have nothing to be sorry for. I understand that that is a past that I had no right to know. And that you don't know or trust me like that yet. So please. Don't apologize for anything."

Bee dropped from the chair and hugged him, burring her face in his shoulder as he quietly soothed her. "That's the reason why I left America. Or was forced to leave. When I didn't give in to what he wanted he slandered me in the papers. My Aunt forced me to move to Scotland."

"Shh. Shh. It's okay, you're alright Bee." He lightly kissed her forehead.

"No, it's not, because why is he here? How did he find me, why would he be in France?"

"Shh it's alright. I'm not sure why he's here. We didn't get that far into our conversation. I." He paused and sighed. "I'll keep him away from you. You won't have to see him."

"Thank you. But you really can't promise me that."

"No, but I'll work my hardest to keep it."

"Thank you."

"There is no need to thank me. It's my job."

"It's your job?"

"Oh, silly Bee. How many times will I have to tell you? I'll keep you safe no matter the cost."

~

"Miss Grey." Beatrice froze at the sound of her maiden name being called. And at the voice of the caller. "Oh, my sincerest apologies. Lady Hashworth." She turned to face him. He didn't look much different; he was still a wolf in sheep's clothing. The only difference was now she was able to see through his façade.

"What do you want?"

"To simply speak with an old friend."

Behind her she heard the tent opening as Edmund appeared. The tension in the air palpable. The small circle of tents that contained his men quieted. His hand touched her back in a comforting movement. It didn't help. "I would rather not speak with you Mr. Jackson."

"My apologies if I have caused offence in some way. However, the reason I wish to speak to you is an urgent matter."

"She has already stated he does not wish to speak with you." Edmund spoke up.

"Do you control your wife's conversations now Captain?" Edmund stiffened beside her.

She needed him to leave before things got any messier. "Mr. Jackson that is not necessary, what do you wish to ask me?"

"Bee." She placed a hand on Edmund's arm quieting him. The sooner Henry asked his question the sooner he would go away.

"I was inquiring if you would mind standing as a physician in a duel I have found myself in?"

Edmund moved to step towards the man. Bee placed a hand on his arm and felt that he was tense beneath her touch. "What are you talking about?"

"Ask you husband. Afterall, he is the one that extended the challenge. I know that you are a good physician," He locked eyes with Edmund and smirked, "among other things. If I fall, I wish for you to care for me. I know that you will treat me with the best care you can and heal my sorrows in every way you can." Bee ignored the comment. Instead, she whipped to Edmund searching his face hoping to find the answer she wanted to. He wouldn't meet her eye. He stared straight ahead at Henry.

"Edmund?" She whispered.

"Mr. Jackson, I think it's time for you to leave."

"Edmund, please?"

"I simply want an answer than I will be on my way. Lady Hashworth?"

Bee was shaking when she turned to him, "Yes alright fine I will do it. Leave." Henry smirked and sauntered off.

She turned, shoving past Edmund to enter the tent.

"Bee-"

"Don't. Don't you dare, you have not a single right to speak right now." She said her voice rising to a yell.

"Bee the things he said I had no choice."

"No choice? No choice? You always have a choice." She refused to look at him. She paced the tent, holding her hands out in front of her has she neared him each turn.

"The things he was saying about you I didn't."

"Yes, you did. For Christ's sake Edmund the one request I have-." His heart tugged as he watched her flip through each nervous motion she had.

"You requested something that I am unable to do." He defended.

"Edmund." She stilled and looked at him.

"No, like I said I am going to protect you no matter the cost. Now listen to me, with the things he was saying he's lucky I didn't run him through right then and there." He approached, reaching out for her when she let him. He lightly grasped her shoulders, "With the things he said I had no choice."

She pulled away from him as he reached to cup her cheek, "Git." and with that she stood glaring at him. Unable to speak any further.

Chapter Fifteen

The silence had returned to crush them yet this time it was a one-sided silence. Edmund had tried to speak with her. Several times. Each time she just ignored him, refusing to look him in the eye. Sometimes he would stop. Other times he would simply continue to speak at her. The duel was tomorrow. A miles ride outside of camp. Edmund had chosen William Parcel to be his second. Henry had chosen some artillery Sergeant. Bee was to be the physician. She hated it. She hated him. Which him she was referring to was unclear to her but she wasn't sure that it mattered in the end.

~

She sat silently behind Edmund. Her hands wrapped around his waist. They rode in silence which was only broken by Parcel asking questions. Questions that received clipped one-word answers from Edmund. Bee felt Edmund tense underneath her hold as the sound of two riders approached. He took one hand and wrapped it around hers. It wasn't to comfort her. He was scared. She was beginning to be too. "I promise that I will never leave you."

"Don't make promises to me that you know you won't keep." It was the first words she'd said to him in days. She flinched. She hadn't meant for it to sound as angry as it did. But it was too late to pull the words back now. Henry and his man approached. He tipped his hat to her. She turned towards the scenery with a grimace.

~

It did matter in the end. And she didn't have to wait long before she had her answer to who she hated. And who she. She. She couldn't lose him not like this. She watched horrified as Henry raised his gun aiming for Edmund. Edmund showed no sign of fear. No sign of wavering. But

Bee did. Oh, did she waver. Her hands clenched in fists, and shook at her side. She watched as Edmund raised his own gun, unblinking. Her breath caught and his eyes flashed to hers. *I promise that I will never leave you.* She decided that she was going to hold him to that.

~

The double crack of the shots ringing out caused her to jump. She was moving before the smoke even cleared. Running to him. She reached Edmund grabbing onto him tightly looking for any signs of injury. He pulled her close giving her a short peck on the forehead. He sighed closing his eyes and bumping their heads together. "I'm alright. I'm alright, go to him." His hand shifted from her cheek to her shoulders as he pushed her away. Towards the man she hated. "He's hurt, go to him." She reluctantly turned away and went.

~

"I hate you."

"I know." He wiped the tears from her cheeks gently. He cradled her head in his hands. The two of them were curled in the cot. Bee clung to Edmund, reassuring herself that he was alive. That he had made it through.

"Don't you ever do that again." She cut him off quickly when he went to speak. "No. I don't care about my honor. I don't care about what they say I don't care about any of it. The only thing I care about." She took a deep breath to calm her tears. "Just please don't do it again." Edmund pulled her closer. Playing with the curl that fell at the center of her face. "Please. Edmund, I have to hear you say it. Promise it. That you won't do it again."

"I swear to you that I will not duel again."

"Thank you. Thank you."

"Bee I. I'm sorry."

"I know. I'm going to hold you to that promise."
"I know."

~

He held her close, as close as he could. The duel had in an odd way brought them back together. Only for a battle to drive them apart again. Or at least pull them apart. The same night of the duel they received word they would march and ride to battle in three days. Now here they were. Edmund and Bee huddled together on the cot. The shells exploding overhead. Edmund was sure that they would never stop. That the shells would always drag him from her side. The same feeling hung in the air. The same as last time. The same as the times before but oh so much worse. He knew. She knew. That the odds of this battle were slim. That they didn't stand a chance at being the victors.

Edmund might not stand a chance at coming back. Bee might not stand a chance at getting out of the small French town alive. His heart squeezed at the thought. He may have promised to never duel again but he would still protect her with his life. He stroked her hair softly. He would try in every way he could to keep her safe.

He looked at her softly. Her eyes meeting his. A shell exploded over head. Without a second thought he leaned in a pressed his lips softly against hers. He felt her gasp before leaning into the kiss. It was not the hurried rough and passionate kisses they had shared before. Kisses filled with lust. No, they moved slowly, kissing softly. The kiss filled with something else entirely. Something that scared Edmund. That scared Bee. But both of them leaned into the fear. Into each other.

He pulled away softly calling her name. He stilled for a moment looking at her. The moment ended far too soon for either of their liking. He pulled her into another kiss this one like their former ones. Rough, passionate. When it ended the both of them rose and prepared for their own battles to come.

They both stood before the entrance of the tent. Neither of them wanting to leave for fear of coming back to find it empty. Silent. She pulled him close and kissed him again. Hoping that it would serve him as well as any confession or prayer she could give him.

Chapter Sixteen

The hospital was chaos. Any patient who could still rise was starting to flee. The medical staff working hard to keep them there. Keep them from injuring themselves further. Bee started when a hand clasped down on her shoulder. She turned half hoping it was Edmund behind her. Instead, she came eye to eye Doctor Monty. "Lady Hashworth you need to go." Beatrice shook her head in protest.

"Sir these men are injured I'm not going anywhere."

"Lady Hashworth, go."

"If you are staying and these men are staying then so am I."

He pulled her from the patient, turning her round to look her full in the eye. "Lady Hashworth, the army is approaching. You are a woman and they will not treat you kindly do you understand?" He shook her slightly, "You must leave. Go!"

"Sir I can't."

"You must!" He pushed her towards the door. Her feet started moving. She knew he was right but with every step she took. Every bed she passed and every man who looked at her as she ran, she felt failure weighing own on her shoulders. The outside of the hospital was eerily quiet compared to the inside. The small town that had become their camp had been abandoned. Only ghosts remained. The dead and the dying.

Bee turned at the sound of her name. She spotted Mr. Parcel riding up the road. She quickly helped him from his horse, careful with his injured leg. "Lady Hashworth you need to leave."

"No I need to help you." She grabbed bandages from her box, pilling them on top of his leg hoping to stop the bleeding.

"Lady Hashworth. Take my horse. Go."

"Not while you're in this condition."

"Please." She looked down at the boy tears gathering in her eyes. She could tell by the look in his face that he already knew that he was bad. "Take my horse. She's tired but still fast."

"I can't."

"You can." She knew no matter how much she hated it that he was right. She quickly tied of the tourniquet hoping that it would buy him just a little more time. Her hands, slippery with his blood grasped his.

"William Parcel, I thank you for being a one true friend to me."

"And I thank you for being mine my lady but please hurry." She nodded and turned boosting herself onto his horse. She rode down the now quiet once bustling road. She forced herself not to look back. It wasn't until she was already a ways down the road before she realized she forgot to ask about Edmund. Her brain told her that Parcel wouldn't leave him if he was still standing. Tears flooded her eyes and she pushed her horse faster.

~

She rode for a full day and a full night. Pushing the exhaustion and tiredness from her brain she rode into the next town.

It was chaos.

The entire army was retreating, all heading to the same place. People flooded the streets looking for loved ones, commanders shouted orders trying the bring order to the chaos. Men ran around desperately searching for friends and brothers. Officers tried to find their missing and scattered men.

Bee pushed all of it from her mind. Riding straight to the hospital. She entered and immediately threw herself back into her work. Patient after patient passed through her hands. All of them with Edmund's face. After the first three she blocked it out. When someone put their hand on her shoulder urging her to sleep, she brushed them off. Calls of her name came from different directions. After a while she stopped turning to see who it was. She stood and her legs gave out from under her. For just a moment she allowed herself to close her eyes.

~

She knew she was dreaming. Or hallucinating. Maybe a bit of both. But she knew that this couldn't be real. She woke up in his arms in a small room. He was holding her to his chest tears streaming from his eyes. She glanced around the room. It was small, similar to hers at the boarding house back in Brighton. A dresser, a vanity, and a bed took up most of the space. He lay in just his undershirt and pants, still dirty from the battle. But he must have changed her. She was no longer in the blood-soaked gown she put on all those days ago. She was in a nightshirt. Not hers or his she guessed by his own state of upheaval. Her hair had also been brushed through and braided. Tears filled her eyes and she turned into his chest.

The small movement alerted him of her consciousness. "Bee? Oh, thank God!" He pulled her even closer crushing her into a hug. "Thank God you're okay."

"I'm okay? You're alive." She rose in an attempt to check him for injury but he was quick to push her back down telling her to rest.

"Stop. Stop. Stop it, lay back. I have already been looked at by a doctor. You need to rest." She looked at him confused, "You collapsed in the hospital. Please just rest." She begrudgingly gave into his request. Settling again on his chest. He let out a small cry, "I thought you were dead. When I arrived in town nobody had seen you. I thought you were still back at the hospital." She held him as he cried. Tears streaming from her own eyes with the relief that he was alive.

"Parcel."

"Parcel?"

"I knew that he wouldn't leave you. Not unless. Unless." She choked on a sob, "When he showed up at the hospital, I thought you were dead." She turned into him sobbing, "Oh Edmund I'm so sorry."

"Sorry?"

"Parcel he was in bad condition, he's still-"

"Bee. Shh. Shh. He's alright, Will. He's alright, he's in the hospital now."

"What?"

"He's alright. I brought him here to the hospital. Someone came in to inform me of his condition only shortly before you woke."

He watched, heart growing, as she broke into a smile. "He's okay?"

"He's okay." She settled again on his chest and they clung to each other as tightly as they could.

After a moment she spoke. "Edmund. Back in the tent-" Bee started. Edmund shifted beneath her and cut her off.

"I'm sorry."

"Sorry?" Bee's face fell.

"I'm sorry because I'm quite positive that I've fallen in love with you." His face was full of anxiety. Not that anyone but her could have told. Anyone but her. She broke into a childish grin. She leaned forward and pressed a light kiss to his nose. Hers wrinkled.

"You need a bath."

"Pardon?"

"You need a bath." She motioned for him to stand "Come on."

Chapter Seventeen

The warmth of the water was heaven to her aching limbs. The warmth of Edmund's chest against her back heaven to her aching heart. She had started to dose of slightly when Edmund moved and began gathering the supplies to shave. She turned in the tub to face him and took the supplies in her hand. "Let me." Edmund raised an eyebrow but surrendered the items in his hands. She carefully applied the shaving cream, mimicking what she had watching him do before. She raised the razor and rolled her eyes when Edmund tensed. "I'm a doctor I have steady hands."

He calmed slightly but not fully. "Watch watch watch." Edmund rose out of the water slightly trying to escape the reach of the straight razor Bee wielded.

"Calm down. I'm not going to cut you."

"Easy for you to be calm you're not the one with the razor at your throat." She carefully dragged the razor up his throat stopping at his chin. He dragged the back of his fingers along the path Bee had cut through the shaving cream. He grinned. "Not quite as close as I normally like."

"Well, it might be a closer shave if you stopped freaking out every time I applied the slightest bit of pressure." He softly took her hand in his and finished shaving.

"See, it's easy."

"Like you were any better your first time." He pulled her close, causing the water to slosh out of the tub.

"I was much better your first time." he teased. She went to smack his chest; he caught her hand. Kissing the back of it. "Oh, honey honey honey Bee."

"Don't. The deal with this bath is that you behave and we both keep our hands to ourselves." He raised an eyebrow at her scolding. "Don't pretend you don't know what you're doing. You only call me that when. Well, when we're. You know." A blush spread across her skin. He considered for a moment before cocking his head to the side and grinning.

"I suppose I do."

"You do so stop it." His hands came to her hips, pulling her flush against his body. She could feel him. His. Excitement. "You promised you would behave. You shouldn't break your promises to your wife."

He had started to kiss down her throat, one hand coming to knead her breast. He grinned as her breath hitched. "I would never break a promise to you. Besides I didn't promise. I said."

"Well, it was still your word and I'm going to hold you to it."

He ground his hips up into hers, "Do you want to hold me to it?"

He lightly teased her clit with his forefinger, grinning up into her neck, "Not if you keep doing that."

"Mm, well then I suppose I should keep it up, shouldn't I?"

She rolled her hips chasing the friction his finger provided. "You should."

She lightly kissed up from his shoulder to his jaw. Nipping along the underside of his jaw. He hummed in pleasure; eyes fluttering shut. He leaned back, lounging in the tub as he slipped his finger into her. Bee's face scrunched in pleasure and she began to roll her hips against him. He pulled his bottom lip between his teeth, enjoying the sight before him. "Honey Bee?" Her breath hitched and he grinned. "Honey Bee." He sung out.

"Stop teasing me."

"Me, tease? Never."

"Is that so?" She leaned forward and grabbed his cock. She lightly wrapped her hand around it, stroking with short teasing jerks.

Edmund's heads fell back, "Well perhaps I do." He groaned. He removed his finger from Bee, pulling her hips flush with his and slowly began thrusting into her. "But I could always be crueler." He stopped rocking as he entered her fully. Holding her hips in an iron grip. She clenched around him breath catching, she let out a high-pitched whine. "Tell me what you want me to do, honey Bee."

"Move. Please." He gave into her request rolling his hips. The water began to slosh out of the tub as his speed increased. He continued to lean back in the tub. Watching. Trying to absorb every detail of the scene he could. Bee sat on top of him breathless and panting. The water moved around her. Her eyes were closed and her head was tilted towards the sky. Her cherry lips opened softly. His own chest heaved as he watched her breasts rise and fall with his thrusts. One hand shifted from her hip to cradle her cheek. She leaned into his touch and opened her eyes. Their eyes met and he felt the knot his stomach tightening. He loved her. Oh he loved her. "Edmund."

"Yes honey Bee?"

"I need you to-" She moaned, "I need you to." His hand had already moved, thumb working quickly at the bud. She fell into his chest as she neared her end. She finished around him, rolling her hips into his, bringing him to his peak soon after. The two sat panting in the tub. The tub was noticeably less full than when they had entered it Bee noted. She would have blushed but she was sure that most of the building was already well aware of what happened the moment Edmund joined her in the bathing room. The toll for marrying a known scoundrel she supposed. She felt his arms tightening around her waist and his breath beginning to even out. She kissed him softly on the nose, his eyes fluttering open. "We can't fall asleep here." He readjusted his grip on her and laid his head back against the metal tub. "Edmund come on, let's head back to the room."

He let out a whine when she stood, laying there for a moment before joining her in gathering their things. They both quickly dressed and returned to the room. He quickly pulled her into bed cocooning the blankets around them both. He fell into his first restful sleep in weeks as he held her there in his arms. He whispered his confession into her scalp. Knowing that not a single thing needed to be said.

Nonetheless his heart jumped when she whispered it back into his chest.

Chapter Eighteen

When someone cornered her in the stairwell, she expected it to be Edmund. She'd expected for lips to be pressed to her neck, hands to slide over her body. She didn't expect the threateningly tight grip. The anger radiating off the person and the voice that was most definitely not her husband's. "I was kind to you. I gave you chance after chance and this is how you repay me? Well Bee," Henry grabbed her chin in an iron grip, forcing her to look at him. "I am done waiting and I am done being kind." She threw her elbow into his chest attempting to push him away. He pressed her further into the wall.

"Get off of me Henry." He grinned, "Get off of me or I will start screaming."

"I will tell. I will tell him; I will tell the papers. I will tell every person I can." He snarled.

"What the hell could you possibly want from me? You've already taken everything you could."

"Isn't it obvious Bee. It's you I have always wanted you." He pressed a vile kiss to her lips, "And oh Bee I have yet to take you."

She yanked her head away, "Get your hands off of me." she struggled in his arms trying to free herself. "I don't want you Henry," She pushed him away. "I never wanted you and I never will. Leave me the hell alone."

"I'll have you because if I don't, I'll tell.

"Then tell you bastard. I don't give a damn."

He threw her back against the wall, "I will tell him and you will lose him. I will make sure you lose everything." He hissed.

"You've already taken everything from me." Bee felt the anger and confidence growing in her chest. Bubbling out. The anger bubbled and replaced the fear that once resided there. "So, take and take again. But you will not have me." He pressed Bee further into the wall and slammed her head back. She grabbed the lapels of his jackets and shoved him back with a shout. She heard a door open at the top of the stairwell but paid it no mind. She pulled her weight to the side in an attempt to throw Henry to the ground. He grasped her hands and twisted her wrists. She cried out and the pain of it, her back hitting the wall once more. She threw her knee up hitting Henry where she knew it would hurt. He struck her across the face and staggered back.

Bee let out a yell and lunged at him. Her anger at the man had finally bubbled over. He had taken everything from her. Her life, her profession. The thing she loved and that gave her purpose. He took everything he could but it still wasn't enough for him. He took it all from her without a second thought. All he did was take. Take for his own selfish wants. She was tired of letting him take. And she would be damned if she let him take the man she loved from her. She lunged.

She felt an arm wrap around her waist. Pulling her back. The back of her head hit someone's chest; she threw her elbow back. Trying to free herself. Hands wrapped around her own, restraining her. Henry looked up at her laughing, "Here comes the man himself. I have something interesting you might want to hear."

Whatever fear of Henry Edmund once observed in Bee was long gone. She struggled against his grip trying to throw herself at the man. "Shut your mouth you bastard. I am tired of you." she shrieked.

"Bee. Bee. Settle down. Bee!" He picked her up around the waist and began to carry her up the steps, back towards their room.

Henry followed the pair slowly. Like an animal that was stalking its prey. "Was it Bernard? Was that it? Yes, Bernard that was the name you used." Bee kicked her legs out. Whether to repel the man or his words Edmund wasn't sure.

"Mr. Jackson leave. Now." He used the same tone he used when giving orders. Hoping that it might get the man to leave for long enough to calm Bee.

"I don't think I will Captain Hashworth. In fact, I'd love the opportunity to speak with you." His focus returned to Bee. Casting a look at her that tempted Edmund to let her go. "That is unless Lady Hashworth accepts my gracious offer."

"Rot in hell you bastard."

"Go! Get out leave before I hit you with more than just a warning shot!" Edmund snarled. He hated this man. He wished for nothing more than to bring him down but his main concern at the moment was his wife. He was going to kill the man for whatever he said to make Bee violent. But first he needed to check to see that she was okay. That she wasn't hurt.

Henry's face twisted into a snarl at the mention of the duel. "I should have shot you dead where you stood." He lunged at the pair. Edmund quickly threw Bee behind him. She slipped under his arms and grabbed Henry's wrist. Her weight brought the both of them tumbling down the stairs. They hit the landing with a crash, Edmund right behind them. Henry had one hand wrapped around Bee's throat the other pinning down one of her arms. Bee's free hand scraped its way down Henry's face. As her hand curled into a fist and his tightened around her throat, Edmund separated the two.

He pulled Bee off of the man. He gathered her into his arms and moved quickly. Getting her as far away from the man before more words that turned into hits could be exchanged. As he climbed the stairs, struggling to keep Bee in his arms, he heard the taunting shouts of "Bernard Young. Bernard Young." Leaving Henry's mouth.

Chapter Nineteen

He locked the door, leaning back against it. A small insurance that Bee wouldn't go barreling back out to beat that man. Not that Edmund would mind. But the outburst was entirely out of character for Bee. And it shocked him. What could Henry have possibly said to make her react that way? "Who's Bernard Young?"

Bee looked up at him from where she sat on the bed, "Me." He raised an eyebrow in question, "Bernard Young was the person I disguised myself as in order to attend university. He was a cousin of mine. Died young. So, I assumed his identity. I wasn't trying to become a physician. Henry wasn't teaching me. I was a physician. I was a doctor. I attended university. I met Henry there. We opened a practice together and I thought everything was good. That everything had worked out. But then one day I got sick. Really sick. I was feverish and completely out of it for months. During that time Henry must have found out. I woke up in a night gown with my bindings gone and Henry sitting next to me. That must have been when he saw my birthmark. He cared for me over the next several days, helped me regain my strength. I thought." She stopped sighing. She stood and began to pace the room her hands fluttering. "I thought he was a friend. He had been a friend he was my friend. I thought that I would get to put my bindings back on. Go back to work. Instead. Instead, the minute I regained my strength he came to me with a proposal. I sleep with him and he won't tell my Aunt. I marry him to keep him from telling the whole world." She paused looking at him with tears in her eyes. "I couldn't do it. I thought he was bluffing. He wasn't. By the end of the day my name was in every scandal sheet every gossip paper in Philadelphia. By the end of the week in every paper in Pennsylvania. By the end of the month every paper in the north east. That's when my Aunt found out and forced me to move to Scotland. I was her responsibility. She hated that, so she planned to marry me off. Hence why I went to Brighton." She looked at him as she stopped speaking. Eyes searching his face for any sign of emotion. His face was blank.

"Okay."

"Okay?"

"Okay. That happened. How do we stop it from happening again?"

"Edmund." She said softly.

He walked to her and cradled her face. "I'm assuming that that bastard wants something. Money, a good word whatever it is we need to stop that from happening again." Her eyes desperately scanned his face, looking for some sort of answer into how he felt beyond saving a reputation. Her eyes met his and they softened. He pulled her into a soft kiss, kissing her nose and forehead before he pulled her into a hug. "Oh my silly little Bee. I love you. Unconditionally. Were you really afraid that what, I would leave you?" Her grip tightened on him as he voiced her fear. "Oh Bee. You don't ever have to worry about me leaving you. Whether you like it or not you're stuck with me."

She placed a kiss on his cheek, "You're very lucky that I like that."

"Believe me I am well aware." He buried his face in her hair, "Now how do we stop that bastard from ruining your life here? What does he want?"

Bee stiffened in his arms, wrapping her arms around his neck, "Edmund look at me." He did albeit confused. "You promised me that you would not duel again and I am going to hold you to that promise until the day that you die do you understand?"

"Bee I-."

"When I tell you we're also going to sit down and find a way to resolve this issue. Understand?"

"Bee-?"

"Do you understand?"

"Yes. What does he want?" She took a deep breath tightening her grip around his neck. As if trying to hold him in place. "Bee. What does he want?"

Her hands fluttered against his back, "He said." She sighed, "He said that he wanted me." A pin could have dropped in that room and been the loudest noise in the world.

"What did he say exactly?"

"Edmund-"

"What did he say. Exactly?"

"He said that. He said that he'll have me. That if he doesn't have me, he'll tell." Edmund moved for the door. Her grip dropped from his neck to his waist. She grabbed the front of his bracers in an attempt to hold him in place. 'Edmund!"

"I'm going to kill that man! That bastard thinks that he can get away with this. I'm going to kill him."

"Edmund please, you said you would stay and that we would talk."

"We have talked. I'm going to kill him."

"Edmund! Sit down right now! We're going to talk about this." His hands came down to grasp hers, his breathing heavy.

"He will not get away with this. He will not."

"He won't but acting in anger is not the right choice. We need to sit down and plan. To come up with something to stop him."

"Fine. Fine. Alright. So, what's your plan?"

She led him to the bed sitting him down, hands on his shoulders to keep him in place. "I'm not positive but I think that I have part of a plan."

His hands came to rest on her hips, "Well then, let's hear it."

Chapter Twenty

"Are you sure these rumors are true?"

"I'm not positive but I tried to keep a tab on all of my former patients. After I was outed and left the practice many of them stopped going. Henry was hurt and needing money so it makes sense. He needed to do something to pay to get here."

Edmund shook his head, stroking his chin as he paced. "I think it is too much of a risk, to walk into this conversation with nothing more than an idea."

Bee threw her hands in the air frustrated. They had gone back and forth for nearly an hour now. Their meeting with Henry was approaching. Fast. "Well it's all we have. Unless you have a better idea" Edmund opened his mouth and Bee quickly cut him off. "No. No. You are not dueling again."

"Fine." Edmund stopped pacing and turned to face her. He only agreed to the not dueling since Bee promised him that if Henry spoke, he could. "You're right it's better than nothing."

"Good. So, we have a plan."

"Part of a plan."

"A plan nonetheless."

He sighed still unconvinced that it was going to work. "A plan."

~

The atmosphere of the room was tense. The three of them sat in the parlor of the former boarding house now turned housing for officers. Due to Edmund's titles Bee and him had been staying there since the battle. Henry had somehow managed to weasel his way into a room.

He currently was sitting across from the two of them. Arrogance coming off him in waves. "So, since you are here, I suppose that means you aware of what I have told your wife."

Edmund's clenched his hand around the arm of his chair. "I am."

"Are you aware of what I'm threatening to tell."

"I am."

"Well, my props to you for being such an understanding husband. That is assuming you aren't here to happily hand over your wife." Edmund moved to rise from his chair stopped by the weight of Bee's hand coming to rest over his. Henry glared disgusted at the point of contact.

"I am not. And I would watch your mouth. I made a promise to my wife not to kill you. However, my patience is beginning to waver"

"I'm not allowed to sleep with another man's wife and you are?"

"I never blackmailed my way into the bed of a woman who didn't want me."

"No from what I've heard you preferred to defile the husband's bed."

"That's enough! From both of you."

Henry turned to her, eyes tracing her body in a way that made Bee's stomach turn. "I suppose you're here to set the rules for our coupling then?"

"There will be no coupling." Both Edmund and Bee said at the same time.

Henry looked confused for a moment before his expression shifted to one of rage and anger. "You do understand what I'm threatening to do?"

"Do you understand that I kept tabs on you?" Bee shot back. "Do you really think I wouldn't know. Patients leaving left and right you needed the money didn't you. But. Oh. No. You weren't taking in the working women and the farm girls. You took in the daughters of the politicians. Their maids. Their affairs. How much did those men pay you? To hid their secrets no matter the mother's will or say in the matter. Enough pay for a ship here I suppose." Henry paled at her words. "I am only going to warn you once Henry Jackson. Revenge is awfully sweet."

"You can't-"

"We can and will do whatever we like, I'm sure the city of Philadelphia would love to have your name in the papers yet again." Edmund added.

"It seems like we're on equal footing here."

"So, it seems."

"Well, I'm sure that there is a solution-"

"There is a solution." Edmund butted in, "A very easy and simple one. You keep quiet about what happened in America and we, well, keep quiet about what happened in America."

Henry fumed for a moment. Eyes frantically searching as he wracked his brain for some, any, information that would give him the upper hand. His faced fell into defeated rage when he realized that he didn't have any.

"Like we said, there will be no coupling." Bee said, her voice strong.

Henry stood quickly and left the room fuming. The door slammed with a bang. Before slamming again as he reentered. "We both stay quiet about what we know. We both go our separate ways."

"We both stay quiet we both go our separate ways." Bee sipped lightly at her tea.

"Agreed." He swept from the room once more. Bee took her first breath in a while. Her face slowly broke into a smile and she turned to Edmund.

"I told you I had a plan. I told you it would work."

"You did." He moved from his chair and kissed her forehead. "That also means that I get to enact my backup plan if necessary."

She sighed, "Yes that means you do." She stood letting him grab her waist and pull her towards him. She placed her hands on his chest fiddling with the cravat. "Yes. Now I have a hospital to get through and you have soldiers to check on."

"A hospital and soldiers I'm sure will understand if we decide to celebrate this victory."

She laughed slightly, "Is there anything else you ever think about."

"Well you can hardly blame me. Nearly a year into our marriage and I'm now just getting to be with you."

"Yet I somehow manage."

"You forget honey Bee. You aren't the scoundrel and rake of this relationship. After all I need to live up to the part."

"Is that the best excuse you can think of?"

"Don't worry love I'm sure that if you give me some time I'll think of some more." He pressed a soft teasing kiss to her lips. As he backed out of the room with her still in his arms. "Come, it'll be quick."

She scrunched her nose, "It never is with you." He laughed and kissed her harder.

Chapter Twenty-One

When she walked into the room, she immediately had 150 pounds of dragoon captain barreling towards her. He swiftly picked her up and spun her around laughing. He leaned down and pressed a chaste kiss to her lips grinning. "What has got you so happy?"

"One that slimy bastard is now out of our lives. And two." He dragged her in the direction of the vanity turned desk. "I just received this." He held a letter in front of her. "It is from my father. He has accepted this marriage as valid and has reextended the financial support of the family to us." He pulled her into a hug, reading the letter over her shoulder. "He has also prepared the summer estate for us and it should be up and operational upon our return from France."

"Oh, Edmund that's wonderful!" She hugged him and kissed him softly.

"It truly is."

"Does this mean that our arrangement has worked out?"

"Yes my love it does."

"Does this mean that we're both free to go?" She teased.

"Don't even joke about that."

She hummed and kissed him softly in apology.

The kisses went from light happy pecks to deeper more passionate ones. Bee's hands found the lapels of Edmund's jacket and pushed him backwards towards the bed. His tongue swept across her mouth, pulling her bottom lip between his teeth. Her fingers quickly worked at the knot of his cravat. Untying it and tossing the length of silk to the side. She propped up on her toes, dragging her teeth down his throat. He groaned, hands squeezing her hips. The back of his legs hit the bed and he fell back on the mattress pulling her on top of him.

He pulled at the fabric of her dress. Bunching it around her hips. She rolled down against him, feeling his growing length through the fabric of his pants. His hands worked quickly, removing her dress and petticoats. When she was left in just her stay and chemise, he rolled her over settling between her legs. His lips traced a path down her neck and across her chest as he pulled at the laces of her stay. Her hands worked at the layers that covered him. Stripping them one by one. He pulled her chemise over her head as she worked his shirt from his pants. He kissed his way down her body as her hands wandered the planes of skin of his shoulders and back. He kissed down the valley between her breasts, stopping to lavish each nipple with his tongue. He continued his way down, kissing the skin at her stomach. The rolls of her hips. He brought his mouth to her knee kissing his way down her thigh. He sucked and bit the skin as he went leaving marks. Her head was thrown back. Her eyes closed. Her mouth opened. Her hands knotted in the sheets.

"Honey Bee." He sang out. His hot breath fanned against her core. She whimpered. "Honey Bee." His tongue darted out, licking a feather light stripe. Her hands flew down to his hair grasping hard. "Honey Bee." She propped up on her elbows, breath catching at the sight before her. Edmund kneeled between her legs, pressing light kisses to her inner thigh. His mouth hung open, his breathing heavy and his eyes blown dark with lust. He grinned when he caught her eye. "Honey Bee, I want you to watch. Can you do that for me?" She nodded. His grin grew, "Good. I knew you could, honey Bee." He didn't waste any time after that. She watched entranced as he began to lick and kiss right where she needed him. His eyes fluttered; he resisted the urge to shut them when he first tasted her. He wanted to watch her fall apart. He grinned. Tongue licking her up and down. She tasted sweet. Like honey. And never before had Edmund been a starving man. But he knew that he would be chasing after that taste for the rest of his life. He didn't spare any part of her. His tongue reached every part of her. He hummed against her and she moaned. Her hands were woven in his dark curls. Her eyes locked with his. Just the way he asked. It wasn't long before she was falling apart, eyes fluttering shut and her head thrown back.

She moaned his name as she finished on his tongue, grinding her hips against him. He wasted no time in ridding himself of his pants and crawling on top of her. He lifted one leg holding her knee in the crook of his elbow. He slipped into her in one smooth motion. Groaning his head fell to her chest as he rutted in her. His moans and whimpers filled the room. The erotic promises began falling from both of their lips. Her head swam in the pleasure that was coming so soon after she had found her peak. She whined and squirmed as he slammed roughly into her. It didn't take long for him to finish. Throwing his head back and calling out "honey Bee." as he did. The two laid there basking in each other's presence, holding one another. "When will we leave France?" Bee asked breaking the silence.

"Hm?"

"You said that there was a house, ready for when we return from France. When will that be?"

"Two years. Maybe a little more maybe a little less. But that's how long my men and I are supposed to stay." He left the unsaid words hanging in the air. The question of if he would survive. His continued reluctance for Bee to be there.

She nodded, "Two years. And we'll have a house waiting for when we get back?"

"Yes. A nice one. It has lovely gardens and big dining and ball rooms." Bee smiled against his chest.

"Tell me more."

"What do you want to know?"

"I don't know. The history, what's happened there. What it looks like."

He smiled and jumped into the history of the house. Going off on tangents, telling the stories of his childhood that took place there.

Chapter Twenty-Two

Within a couple of months more exciting mail had arrived. As soon as Edmund saw the sender, he rushed to find Bee. He rushed back to their tent. The army had continued to march in that month. The two had also grown closer. It was terrifying. To them both, to fall for someone in a place where things could so easily be ripped away. But neither of them would exchange what they had for security. They had fallen in love. It had been a slippery and intense slope for the both of them. Which is why Edmund's news would be so exciting. She may be angry at him but he hoped to opportunity it provided would outweigh that. Flinging the flaps open. She sat at the desk writing in notebook with her med box open. "Hello?" She watched as he broke into a boyish grin.

"Hello."

"Is everything alright?" He stood before her breathless and smiling.

"Why yes, everything is alright. Why wouldn't it be?" She raised an eyebrow. He tossed the letter her way. He watched her face as she read over it shifting nervously from foot to foot. When she was finished reading, she carefully refolded the letter a placed it on the desk. She smiled up at him. He hoped that was a good sign.

"Why?" His grin fell slightly.

"Because it gives you the chance to be a physician again. Or, like a physician."

"I'm not leaving." She repeated part of their agreement from months ago.

"I know you aren't. But." He sighed, he knelt in front of her and took her hands in his. "I love you. I don't want you to leave. And I know why you have to be here. But I thought maybe. Just maybe you could do it there."

"Edmund." She stroked his cheek.

"Almost every soldier and sailor that comes back passes through that hospital. It's in London. My family has a townhouse that you would stay in. Right now, the hospital is understaffed. When I wrote to the lead physician, he was ecstatic that they might gain someone with your training and education."

"My training and education?"

"That's the thing Bee, you aren't going there as a nurse you're going there as a physician. A surgeon. They know that you went to university. That you have the training, experience and education to do the job."

"Edmund-"

"Look I know-" She placed a finger over his mouth quieting him.

"Edmund I'm going to take this opportunity. I'm going to go. This is perfect timing."

"Perfect timing for what?"

Her hands fluttered and his concern grew, "I need to leave soon anyway."

"Is everything alright? Is your aunt alright? Did that bastard Jackson not keep his word?"

"No, no it's none of that." She smiled softly and took his hand. "Edmund I'm in the family way." She watched as his brain stopped working for a moment before kicking into overdrive. As his face went from confusion to blankness to pure joy. He moved forward, grabbing her from her chair and sweeping her into a hug.

"You are?"

"Yes."

"Oh I. OH." He began laughing as he spun her in a circle.

"Edmund! Edmund put me down."

"Oh." He dropped her, quickly and pulled her into a tight hug, cradling her head. Tears filled his eyes as he held her. He was glad he took the risk of writing.

~

Two months later the two. Three. Of them stood on a crowded dock. At Bee's feet sat her medical box and small traveling tote. Her trunk had already been loaded on the ship. "Write to me." She softly caressed Edmund's face soothing the worry lines with her touch.

"Of course I will."

"I want to know about everything that happens."

"You'll hear it all. Don't worry." She smiled, "At the end of each day I'll sit down in the grand house and write what happened that day. Minute by minute." She joked.

He smiled, "Good. I expect nothing less." His hand shifted to her stomach, resting atop the small bump that had started to form. He looked down slight tears forming in his eyes.

"Stop you, aren't allowed to be the one crying."

He smiled as tears began to roll down his cheeks. "And why's that. I'm the one saying good bye to my wife and child."

"Because." Her voice broke slightly, "Because we're the ones that are going to be safe."

He grinned again finding her eyes, "I know. But. I know."

"But what?"

"It's selfish but I want you to be here by my side."

"And I'd rather you be by mine. And besides," Her hand came to cover his, "We have nothing to worry about. We'll spend day in and day out surrounded by doctors and nurses. And if your sister is as half overbearing as you make her out to be then I'm sure I won't be moving a single muscle once I'm done at the hospital."

"She is exactly as overbearing as I have made her out to be." The both of them looked up as there was a last call for boarding the ship. "Be safe. Keep me updated."

"I will, I will. She kissed him hard as though it may be her last time. She grabbed her things and began to walk up the gang plank.

"Bee! I'll send you baby names in every letter." Edmund called walking beside her as she made her way up.

"I'm holding you to that promise love!" She yelled down at him. Sailors rushed around her as the ship began to drift into the sea. She stayed at the railing, wiping tears rapidly from her eyes.

"You'll know how to find my sister?!"

"You've described her enough I could find her with my eyes closed!"

"Good!" She stayed standing at the rail until Edmund was nothing more than a small red dot in thousands. She stayed, despite the sailors protests until the dock disappeared over the horizon. Tears in her eyes and her hand on her stomach. He would come back. He needed to come back. Behind she heard the sound of a rope snapping and something falling. A man cried out. She lifted her box. Her work began.

THE END
TC Camille © 2020

Don't miss out!

Visit the website below and you can sign up to receive emails whenever TC Camille publishes a new book. There's no charge and no obligation.

https://books2read.com/r/B-A-DEZQ-GSSTB

BOOKS 2 READ

Connecting independent readers to independent writers.